Mckenna of Dreams and Substance

Mckenna of Dreams and Substance

Joszann St. John

Copyright © 2010 by Joszann St. John.

Library of Congress Control Number: 2010915535
ISBN: Hardcover   978-1-4535-9913-6
         Softcover   978-1-4535-9912-9
         Ebook   978-1-4535-9914-3

All rights reserved. No part of this book may be reproduced or transmitted in any form or by any means, electronic or mechanical, including photocopying, recording, or by any information storage and retrieval system, without permission in writing from the copyright owner.

This is a work of fiction. Names, characters, places and incidents either are the product of the author's imagination or are used fictitiously, and any resemblance to any actual persons, living or dead, events, or locales is entirely coincidental.

I would like to acknowledge the use of two websites.
Government of Prince Edward Island *www.gov.pe.ca*
City of Toronto *www.toronto.ca*

This book was printed in the United States of America.

To order additional copies of this book, contact:
Xlibris Corporation
1-888-795-4274
www.Xlibris.com
Orders@Xlibris.com

DEDICATION

To all the women of the world, those that have gone before me, your lessons haven't been forgotten. Your beauty remains in the legacy of humanity. To my Mom Erma, my grandmother Ruth and all the women who have contributed to my life.
You know yourselves!

Part I

Chapter 1

It was two hours past noon on a Wednesday afternoon. Mayjean Samuel, her red hat askew on her head, sat in her usual spot under the shade of the Long mango tree. The tree stood some distance from the painted brown and white of Mayjean's house. Every day at this time, regular, without fail, her crochet needles kept pace with her nimble fingers, creating patterns and designs passed down from a long line of Samuel matriarchs. The Samuel women had an illustrious history with the crochet, with each successive generation, the passing of the crochet baton was tradition, a little piece of family history. A special relationship existed between Mayjean and her brightly colored threads. Threads that were neatly kept in a worn terry cloth bag, never far from her side. Now as she sat in total relaxation, multicolored hues overflowed and spilled out in every direction as they lay nestled in her lap.

The magic of the crochet lay in the creation of stunning visual masterpieces. Over the years, Mayjean's needles had become her best friends, keeping her company through bereavements, broken friendships, hurricane storms and the many trials of a life lived. Crochet was life, a calming pastime, a source of income, and a soothing comfort. Many nights when she was sleepless and lonely, like a diligent lover, crochet kept the ugliness at bay, bad memories and restless fingers forgotten in the pursuit of the next pattern.

Mayjean had given up on her dreams long ago. Her granddaughter McKenna was the only bright light in her days now. Death had come unannounced to Mayjean, the kind of death that thrives on half empty. Infinite promise now lived in a burnt out, hollowed husk, walking in the shadows of dreams unfulfilled. As a young woman, unharnessed and untapped raw potential energy had been diverted. What poverty had left intact, unrequited love had stolen, like a thief in the dead of night, and had lain to waste. Mayjean's saving grace had been the natural environment. She had always felt connected to nature. Each time she bathed at Swallow's Point her favorite beach, it was as if she was soaking up strength from the Caribbean Sea. She would sit for hours just day dreaming and letting the cool water flow over her. The wind through her hair and on her skin descended like a calm benevolent spirit pouring out a sweet salve.

Like today where she sat in quiet repose on the embankment. She was content in this moment. A slight breeze ruffled the leaves of the mango tree. Its branches laden with ripe fruit, some were hanging down within arm's reach. Children and passersby would stone the tree while standing in the street and would whoop with delight when a ripe mango would come down. Mayjean's mangoes were sought after in mango season; it was rumored that they were the sweetest in the village. Children going to and from school, or doing errands in the shop for their mothers, found themselves under the tree. Being a weekday most children had gone back to school for the afternoon. Except for the occasional vehicle passing through the village of Chantilly, silence hung quietly.

From her vantage point, Mayjean could see everyone who went by. Poised and unruffled she commanded respect. A fixture in the village, her word was law. She had borne her trials with rare dignity; she never railed at life. She liked to sit in the afternoons and see people going about their business. Bepto, a jack-of-all-trades but master of none, came up the street, with a bag perched on his head. In the heat of the afternoon, sweat poured down his dark bronzed face in an unbroken line.

"Hey, Mayjean, ah wa go an tiday."

"You got it going on, Bepto, ah wa mi dat," replied Mayjean.

"You bag heavi sah."

"Som pempere mi pik up dong daye by Alfred."

"Okay, sah." Under her breath Mayjean whispered, "The nerve! Thieving, son of a gun." She remembered a time when Bepto's father, Sandman, walked the streets in the same manner. The apple doesn't fall far from the tree, she thought. Bepto was always in somebody's business; insults never deterred him.

After Bepto went on his merry way, Ursula, the village drunk, and little Benji went by. Ursula had no special time of day to get drunk; she was a disgrace to her children and family. Many a time she had to be helped home because her legs, unsteady from the bottle, would not cooperate. On the weekends, she drank from sunup to sunset, and her partying knew no bounds.

Friday was payday. Standing in line at the banana-boxing plant, Ursula wore a silly grin on her face. Her grin was cut short when she came from the line and she had to go with her mother and daughter to change her paycheck. If her mother did not intervene, her children would have starved for sure. Ursula, like many others in the village, had worked hard when banana was king. Most people had earned a good living then. Now the economy was in shambles. Ursula's drinking was in part a coping mechanism. It was depressing, finding money to feed and clothe a houseful of children. In Chantilly those who found steady employment faired better than most. Villagers and most of the island now relied heavily on the service and tourism industries as a source of income.

Drunks, men and women alike, created quite a spectacle and provided much humor in Chantilly. Ursula was a tiny wizened woman of about five four. Her skin had become leathery from sun and alcohol abuse. Hair once black and shiny now hung limp and was usually tied back into a bun. Kind brown eyes that were once creased in open smiles looked into the world now with scorn and derision. It was as if Ursula came alive only on the weekends, when she left her five children with her mother and she shared kinship with the bottle.

Music and Caribbean rum went hand in hand in Chantilly. Occasionally there would be a village *blocko*, or big dance, on the weekend. Loudspeakers would blast music; the usual suspects would be the Mighty Sparrow Calypso songs or Bob Marley's reggae tunes. Sometimes Sparrow's "Jean and Dinah" would often spill out into the streets, and the alcohol-laden hips would gyrate, keeping time with the music. Ursula would be in her element then; she would dance and curse like a hurricane had come upon her. One of her drinking buddies was Tom Theodore. He made sure you knew who he was after one of his binges. He would stand in the streets swaying, staggering, and beating his chest. In his best drunken drawl, he'd say, "I am Tom Theodore. Everybody loves me." Then his buddy Ursula would high-five him. Their act had grown stale though, but they continued, unawares.

Mayjean was fond of little Benji. Benji, a boy of six, showed great promise to come. He was a fast learner, and Mayjean took pride in his accomplishments as he always excelled in school. The older woman would save treats and mangoes for him. Today like every other time the little boy was full of excitement.

"Mayjean!" shouted Benji.

"Come, child, I got something for you," said a happy and jovial Mayjean.

"Go in the corner of the porch. You see the bag there. Take it to your mother."

"Thank you so much, MamaJean." Benji knew there was something in it for him; he took off, running as fast as his little legs would carry him.

The boy's father had left before he was born. The news came that he had started another family overseas in one of the neighboring islands. Claudia, Benji's mother, was a strong woman who reminded Mayjean of a younger version of herself. Claudia eked out a living planting a vegetable cash crop garden. She was extremely fond of Mayjean because of the extras the woman provided for her three children and herself. Life was a challenge for Claudia, but she did a good job of raising little Benji.

Time passed slowly. Children on their way home from school after the four o'clock hour signaled that the afternoon was coming to a close. In the later months, night always came early to Chantilly. Mayjean thought she had better start making preparations for supper. She had left McKenna reading one of her many books, curled up in dasheen, bananas, and plantains were placed on the ground beside the low wall where they sat. Their talk soon turned to village gossip. The blowing of a conch shell signaled that the van carrying the catch of the day had arrived.

The crowd converged around the van as loud and excited voices started calling out "one pound of fish . . . two pounds jack . . ." It was a melee, and Mayjean was smack in the middle. Boysie called out to her to come forward. He always gave Mayjean extra fish. At one time they had been lovers. Mayjean had just come from the road when an anxious Bepto knocked on her door. "Mamajean . . . Mamajean . . . they want for you to come now."

"Ah wa . . . happen?"

"Well, Christina fall sick. They . . . rushing her to the hospital."

Mayjean's unhurried "nothing nuh wrang wid she" made Bepto pull up short.

"I don't know, Mamajean. They just send me."

"She mus be pregnant again."

"Ah yu oh! Mi pooh pickni."

"Okay wait . . . mea come." Her fish broth would have to wait. She chucked the fish in the refrigerator in anger. Mayjean took her time finding her clothes. Every time her daughter got pregnant, she always ended up in the hospital. This time she had enough; it was time Christina took stock of her own life. She was sick and fed up with bailing her out.

"McKenna, chile, your mother in di hospital. Come let us go and see wah wrong wid she," said Mayjean, getting more agitated by the minute.

Mayjean had birthed seven children; two were now deceased. Tiny Tim had not been born a month when he passed on. The other child, Julius, had a run in with the police due to gang violence. His mother still wept for him these past twenty years. Some of the other children had immigrated to Canada and to America.

McKenna's mother, Christina, or Tina to some, still lived in Chantilly. She had been the most difficult of all Mayjean's progeny. Christina had come into the world kicking, screaming, and yelling at the top of her lungs. Now at thirty-eight, her loud personality was legendary. Some people never changed no matter what happened to them. She refused to learn from her mistakes, living on the outskirts of Chantilly in a house full of her children. Fatherless denizens as she herself once was.

Raising children was a challenge in itself, but Tina had given new meaning to the word *difficult*. Some of Mayjean's gray hairs were attributed to her. Even in childhood and as a young woman, Tina did what she always wanted. Threats and spankings were lost on her. A mistress of swear words by the time she was ten, she cursed at any and everybody. Hellion was a mild term to describe her; her name was known throughout the village and even in the city.

Tina, at eight, had cursed at Bepto. She had run of by herself to see the candidates of the political parties campaigning in the streets. "Go home, little gwal ah, waye yu modder daye" he had chided. To which she had replied, "Man, ah non mi yo tak to, so shut up. Nuh ask me no question."

One year, at Christmas time, she had cursed at the village postmistress when she told Christina go on right home with her mother's mail. Mayjean had to stop sending Christina to buy groceries in the village shop. She either stole the money to buy candy or took so long her mother would have to come find her. On other occasions, she would stop to play or go on her own errands with her friends. The Dell's shop incident was a turning point in Tina and Mayjean's relationship.

Tina was about eleven when she was sent to Dells shop to buy chicken for their dinner. Her friends were on their way to the beach, so she forgot about the chicken and took off with them. Six hours passed with no sign of the little termagant. That was the first night Christina slept away from her mothers house. Mayjean had been furious at her daughter's wanton disregard and disobedience, and forbade her from coming through her door. She had to find lodging in her aunt's house that night. For many years, Christina's escapades brought shame and scandal to the Samuel household. Mayjean was at her wits end; she hadn't known what to do with her daughter. It seemed a part of Christina had been tuned off; she was deaf to the pleas of Mayjean begging her to change her ways.

Mayjean had blamed herself for Christina's rebellion. Maybe if Anthony had stayed, things would not have been so difficult. Over the years, she had no problems finding his replacements. Part of her wanted to show Anthony and the Serrant family that she didn't need them. She was young, and good looks and a fine form had men lining up to be her paramours. Mayjean had often wondered if it was the companionship she craved, or if it was something more. She never really understood men. After Anthony, she had to become independent; she had grown up fast.

Mayjean had sometimes worked in Ma Dulcie's shop, especially when Dulcie went on her shopping trips to St. Marteen or to America. Mayjean's mother, Agnes, had been a great help to her while she raised her children. After Anthony, she had erected walls to barricade her heart. No one would ever see her bleed like that again. She loved from a distance; it was as if part of her had been cauterized. Her lovers could never penetrate that core that was locked away. They knew better; if they pushed for more, they would be out in the cold. Most didn't care anyway. They were happy with what they got, so they never complained too much.

Hospitals had never been Mayjean's favorite places. There was something strange about dying and giving birth in the same place. She had always associated hospitals with pain and ugliness. If she could avoid it, she stayed far away from doctors and their place of business. It didn't help that she had to identify Julius, her firstborn son, in the hospital after he had died. Her precious mother, Agnes, had spent her final days heavily sedated in the big hospital in the city. It had just broken her spirit to see her mother lying so helpless. Mayjean had always been her own doctor, until now. She had helped McKenna and many others in Chantilly get over illnesses. Her healing capabilities and knowledge of bush medicine and natural remedies had proven invaluable on many occasions.

Christina was taken to Barnes Hospital, a small country hospital located some six villages away from Chantilly. The hospital had been named after some missionary who had come to the island

and had helped to build up the surrounding villages. The smell of disinfectant, decay, and the underlying heaviness of sickness hung in the air. In the hospital corridor, intermittent groans and cries could be heard coming from some of the rooms. Bepto stayed with Mayjean and McKenna the whole time. He had gotten a ride for them because the ambulance had long gone with Christina.

The nurses' station was located in the front section of the hospital. A beaming young nurse attired in the obligatory white starched uniform was the solitary occupant of the booth."

"Hello . . . can I help you?" asked the nurse.

"Yes," said Mayjean. I'm looking for my daughter."

"What's her name mam?"

Bepto nudged Mayjean in her side. "Christina," he whispered in an undertone. Mayjean deep in thought and distracted had to be nudged a few times by Bepto as he tried to bring her back to the present.

McKenna stayed silent looking on; she had been through this before, and had become detached from her mother's suffering.

"Uh . . . okay. She's in room 112, right down the hall."

Not many people loitered in the hallway. One cleaning attendant was bent over mopping a small section of floor. Two other individuals, who looked like visitors, bobbed their head in greeting as they passed Mayjean, McKenna, and Bepto.

The white walls and white furnishings always unnerved Mayjean. She was a woman who loved color. What little color there was came from the flower-patterned drapes separating the rooms, and the flower arrangement on one of the small tables in a room they passed. The outside heat hadn't penetrated the inner sanctum of the building. Apart from the occasional cries of suffering, the only other sound came from three overhead fans whirring at a furious pace, dispatching a cooling breeze.

Mayjean hadn't seen Christina in five days. She was shocked to see her daughter's withdrawn hollow eyed appearance. Her dark brown skin had a dull tinge, and a small grimace sat atop her ashen face. Intravenous drips were feeding nourishment into her veins. During her pregnancies, Christina suffered from extreme hyperemesis, a condition that caused extreme nausea and vomiting usually in the early trimesters. In Tina's case, she was ill throughout most of the pregnancy. Mayjean often wondered why Christina wasn't more vigilant about pregnancy. Christina's other daughter, Grace, sat at her bedside holding onto her mother's hands.

"Christina, what's wrong wid you this time?"

"Mama, well, you know."

"Grace, McKenna, and Bepto, step outside a while please." said an angry Mayjean.

Grace never said a word, but if looks could kill, her grandmother would have dropped dead in that instant.

"So, Christina, you pregnant again," said Mayjean in a hushed voice, not wanting the occupants of the other room to hear her business.

"Mama, I . . . I don't know how it happened"

"After six pickni, yu don't know how it happens," hissed a frustrated Mayjean. "Yu mad gwal, yu nuh tired bring shame ah mi eye. When you gonna stap? Ah pickni yu want so. Yu nea put water ah yu wine. Enough is enough. Who gonna help you dis time? My health is not what it used to be. I am getting old. Yu love misery, eh. You can't even take care of your other children, why would you have more? I don't understand yu."

By this time, Christina was bawling her eyes out. "I know, Mama, but it just happened."

"How far along are you?" said Mayjean, looking at her stomach. "You look about six months or thereabouts. You fool me this time," said Mayjean. "That's why you stayed away and you were wearing all those big clothes."

"Well, the doctor says I about five and a half months along," said a tired Christina.

"Well, who is it this time?" asked a visibly frustrated Mayjean.

"Yu not going to like it, so its better you don't know who it is, he's helping me out."

"Waye him daye then?"

"He's working in the garden."

"Mi hope ah not that drifter yu name eh call with." Christina had started to clam up, but then she regained some of her composure. Back in control of herself, she replied, "Mayjean, don't worry, It will work out this time, you'll see."

"What about your doctor bills?" "Look, you getting sick already." "Everything costs so much money these days." "I helped you for so long, Oh God!" Mayjean was shaking her head.

Mayjean looked at her daughter, her firstborn. She had been so proud when she gave birth to her all those years ago. So much had happened between them, she sometimes wished she could have spared Christina some of life's heartaches. Brown eyes, identical pools of liquid honey, stared back at each other. Mayjean was moved to gently stroke her daughter's cheek. Something she never did ever. Her anger was tempered by a sudden understanding of her daughter's nature. It was the same beast that had ridden her when she was younger. Her maternal instinct and compassion took over, and she pitied her daughter. God help Christina because there was nothing more she could do for her. Mayjean had never gotten married, and she had wanted that for Christina. Tina had followed in her footsteps; she had multiple lovers over the years. Of Tina's six children, only three shared the same father.

The past had repeated itself once again. Mayjean herself had gotten pregnant with Tina when she was eighteen years old and still living under her mother's roof. Tina hadn't done much better; it just broke her heart to see her firstborn so lost. She had done the best by her children, giving each child a fair amount of love. Her mom, Agnes, had helped. She had been a major source of strength. At one point, both women had taken turns working in the banana fields. Bananas required a lot of effort; from planting to harvesting, the process took about ten months. Pruning and feeding each plant had to be done efficiently to ensure optimum results. It had been hard work until the bananas matured. During those years, crochet too had helped put food on the table.

Mayjean blamed herself, but all the blame in the world would not erase the past. She often asked herself what more she could have done. She had made peace with the past these last years. Anthony Serrant, Christina's dad, had little to do with them. When Tina was younger, he had an active role in their lives, but his involvement had waned with each intervening year.

Chapter 3

Mayjean had known Anthony Serrant all of her life. They were relatively close in age; Anthony was only a few years older. He was educated at St. Mary's Academy in the city while Mayjean went to the public school in the village. The Serrants were the dominant family in Chantilly. They had owned most of the land and business holdings in the village and surrounding countryside. Like most people of means, they controlled the majority of the resources and established their own social mores. Even though Chantilly numbered about seven thousand, the Samuels and the Serrants did not move in the same circles.

Chantilly was the by-product of the colonial era. Remnants of the Caribbean's history with slavery lingered on in the island, and cultural distinctions were woven into the fabric of society in many subtle ways. The village people were mostly descendants of African slaves, though there were the odd European doctor or clergy living among them as missionaries. Like most communities, a hierarchy existed in the Chantilly. Delineated lines between the have and have-nots had existed with the creation of free villages after emancipation from slavery. Depending on their station in the plantations, some slaves, upon being freed, were able to obtain property, which afforded them a better start in their new life. People like the Serrants looked down on those who were not as wealthy, like the Samuels.

The Serrant story began back in the dark days of slavery, when the St. Baptiste Estate on Belantine came into French hands after the British lost a skirmish with the French in the late 1700s. Pierre Serrant the Elder was already in poor health when he took over the estate. He sent for his son, Charles, who had just married and had left his young wife behind in France. Upon arriving in Belantine, Charles was immediately smitten with the slave girl Luella. Her angelic black skin was a sharp contrast to the women he had known before. Luella was as beautiful as she was intelligent. Before long, she was ensconced in the big house as Charles mistress. He then granted her freedom. Luella lived with Charles and enjoyed privileges unknown to the other slaves on the estate. Charles took over from his father and lived almost exclusively on Belantine. His wife came to visit once. By this time, Luella had given birth to two of Charles progeny. Charles was in love with Luella and totally ignored his wife, who went back to France and never set foot on Belantine again.

It was Luella and Charles's progenies that had started the Chantilly Serrants. The Serrants had owned the first village shop. People said they were wealthy because they had sold their souls to the devil. The Serrants, apart from being wealthy, had been endowed with much physical beauty passed on from their mixed heritage. The Samuels, on the other hand, had come from a long line of laborers and had moved up the social ladder by their community service. For many generations Chantilly women had competed and flaunted themselves in the hopes of marrying a Serrant. The men always took lovers but never married village women.

Anthony came home to Chantilly on weekends and all other holidays to be with his family. It was during those times that he and Mayjean cultivated their friendship. Sometimes they would meet at Sunday service as both families attended the Roman Catholic Church.

Anthony's mom, Hilda, was a robust woman. She had money, and she wasn't ashamed to broadcast it. Her clothing choices were often of the loud and ill-fitting kind. Hilda's nose was permanently tilted up to the sky; it was as if she was breathing rarefied air no one else was allowed to partake of. Over the years, she would cast surreptitious glances over at Mayjean when she saw her with Anthony. Hilda believed the village women were not good enough for her sons. It was no secret that she preferred living in the city. Old Serrant had stood firm; he had always lived in the country, and no woman would change his mind. He had compensated by buying a second house in the city. Hilda had the best of both worlds. People in the village often wondered why she had married a country boy. They speculated she had married him for his money, and her love was of the mercenary kind. Hilda's husband was good to the village people; he had provided jobs through his businesses and would lend many a helping hand.

Mayjean's ancestors and the Serrants had tangled before, and Samuel blood had been spilled. About four generations removed, a Samuel man and a Serrant woman had fallen in love. The Serrant family had been against the union. One night some members of the Serrant clan had lain in wait, ambushed, and beaten up the unlucky suitor. The woman had been sent to live with an aunt in a neighboring island, which effectively destroyed any chances they might have had.

Mayjean and Anthony's friendship continued on for many years. During the onset of puberty, she wasn't exactly sure when, things started changing between herself and her best friend. The first glimmers of awareness between male and female became more apparent the more they saw of each other. The lovers couldn't wait to be in each other's company. Agnes, Mayjean's mother, had given long lectures on the pitfalls of dating Anthony and warned her daughter about getting pregnant. Mayjean was told over and over. But did she listen? Oh no! They spent all of their time together; they were young and in love. Mayjean felt she had the best chance of becoming Mrs. Anthony Serrant. She had everything going for her—beauty, intelligence, and a nice figure. To top it off, Anthony was in love with her. The other village girls were jealous and threw hateful glances her way; she ignored them all. No one would steal her joy, not even Hilda. It was a glorious time in her young life. Anthony spent less time in the city; he came home to Chantilly to be with her. Hilda did not like the situation one bit. She tried many subtle tactics to separate the lovers. Her smiles reeked of falsity and were becoming stiffer than starched crinoline.

Young love had persuaded and beguiled Mayjean daily. Her dreams of studying to become a doctor grew dim with each passing moment in Anthony's presence. Soon clandestine meetings, long walks, and innocent touches led to the full expression of their love. Mayjean's periods had stopped suddenly, and her real fears were realized. She had become pregnant with Christina; her mother's predictions had come true. Mayjean felt for sure Anthony would marry her then, but she didn't realize the power Hilda wielded. Even though Anthony was a young adult, he lived in his parent's home and was subject to their wishes. Hilda, upon hearing of the pregnancy, stated it could not be her son's. She invented names of the many men Mayjean had been with. She said Anthony was too young to be a father; she had bigger plans for her son. A financial agreement was agreed upon to help Mayjean with the raising of the child, and Anthony was sent away to finish his education. He came back after being gone two years and became the agricultural supervisor for the district.

During that time, Christina had been born and was in her second year. Mayjean's relationship with Hilda had not improved even after the birth of the baby. Both women resented each other; their dislike for each other provided much gossip in the village. Mayjean's relationship with Anthony became troubled and disintegrated eventually. She had blamed him for not standing up to his mother for her. One day after church, Mayjean was crossing the street and Hilda was on the other side. Hilda had looked directly at Mayjean and had spat on the ground, showing her distaste for the other woman. That had been the final straw, and Mayjean had washed her hands off the family and moved on.

Now looking back, Mayjean remembered her struggles. It wasn't easy but she had survived, and she was stronger than she had ever thought back then. Her children had all grown up. The four that lived overseas sent her some money monthly, and her crochet brought in some income. She sold the pieces in the market in the city, and down at the community center, she got a small fee for teaching the young women her skill. She had her mother and grandmother to thank for teaching her. Mayjean remembered a time when she did not want to be bothered with crochet. With the money McKenna made working at the credit union, she did not have to work so hard anymore. She did not trust the girl going to the city to work by herself. Mayjean knew the pitfalls that waited for the unsuspecting youth. The young always felt invincible, only to be brought up short when the inevitable happened. Her logic was, if you played with fire, you should expect to get burned.

Chantilly did not figure in Mayjean plans for McKenna; she wanted the best for her granddaughter. Everything that time had denied her would be McKenna's. McKenna was by far the most accomplished Samuel ever. Poverty and bad choices had stolen Mayjean's dreams. McKenna was a bright light; her future shone bright. Surely she was born for great things; her beauty and intelligence was unparalleled in Chantilly. Mayjean had been getting visions for a long time now. From her birth, McKenna had always been special. Mayjean had looked into the red-puckered and wrinkled face of the newborn McKenna and knew she would protect with her dying breath this first grandchild. She had always loved her as her own. Christina was all too glad to give her up because she had been young and not wanted the responsibility. Even as a child, McKenna was always bubbly and inquisitive. As a toddler, she had followed everyone in the house on chubby legs that never walked but ran. She had always been Mayjean's pride and joy.

Christina's pregnancy had thrown Mayjean. It was not news she wanted to hear, so close on the heels of her own visit to the doctor. Mayjean was comforted by McKenna's levelheadedness. Christina and McKenna were like night and day, similar yet different. Where Christina was willful, McKenna was inquisitive. Mayjean had been able to keep McKenna fairly occupied so far with books and tutored piano lessons. That had been temporary; womanhood was calling to McKenna. Fragile cracks had started appearing in their relationship, creating tension and straining the bonds of familiarity and obedience. McKenna was like a wild horse scenting freedom but unwise of the perils of too much too soon.

It was Chantilly's annual fair day. A huge green tent was set up in the old school grounds. Most of the villagers, especially the young, turned out for the games, food, and music. The fair always culminated in a huge bonfire. For days the men had created a pyramid-shaped structure of wood, lashed through with rope. Mayjean could hear the whoops of the crowd that signaled the lighting of the structure. This year she had stayed home. The excitement was at odds with her mood. She had suggested McKenna should go on without her.

Watching from behind her white lace curtains, she was dismayed to see McKenna and Brian strolling down the street. Mayjean's blood boiled. She now realized Brian was up to his usual tricks. Many of the young girls in the village had fallen for his charms. Brian was a user; he had one serious relationship that had just ended. Up until now, there was never any reason for Mayjean to get involved in Brian's affairs. Where McKenna was concerned though was a different matter. Mayjean's anger propelled her outside onto her front porch. Her sudden appearance caused two collective gasps from the young couple caught up in conversation.

Brian's surprise turned into a sneer of derision. McKenna was still wearing her shocked grimace. She knew Mayjean had talked about Brian advances, and she had brushed it off as friendly neighborhood banter. By Mayjean's scowl, she knew the jig was up. How she hated to be caught.

"Mamajean, you waited up. You shouldn't have. I would be fine you know. I thought you're not feeling well."

"I had one of my teas," replied Mayjean. "So, Brian, how was the fair?" asked a seething Mayjean. Mayjean was keeping a tight lid on her temper; she did not want to embarrass McKenna anymore than she had too.

"Oh! Good! Mamajean, one of the best yet."

Yes! You think you found an easy target. Oh no, not dis time, boy, thought Mayjean.

Brian's white teeth gleamed like a shark in the near dusk. He had no problems finding women. He couldn't figure out McKenna yet, but he knew he wanted her. In his experience, they always said yes eventually. He thought Mayjean was just an old woman.

What can she really do to me? She can talk all she want, but she can't stop me, thought a belligerent Brian.

McKenna watched the wordless interplay between the two combatants and rushed in to diffuse the developing situation.

"Brian, I will see you, okay?" McKenna hurried Mayjean into the house. She was in for an earful. Alone she could handle Mayjean. She didn't need the whole world in on her affairs. Anger could unleash another side of Mayjean she didn't need right now. Brian watched McKenna go. She would be his. He would make sure of it.

Chapter 4

Silence reigned for the next couple of days in Mayjean's house. McKenna did her best not to annoy her grandmother any further. Mayjean had quarreled far into the night after the fair. She told McKenna that Brian was nothing but trouble. McKenna loved her grandmother dearly, but she wasn't a child anymore. She could fight her own battles. It was time Mayjean started realizing that. Lately this feeling of restlessness haunted her quiet moments. She was waiting for something, but she didn't know what that was. She had grown up in this house, yet she felt the walls closing in on her. Last night she had those dreams again. After the dream, she always woke up with her clothes drenched in perspiration, and her heart would beat uncontrollably until Mayjean gave her one of her teas.

She waited for Beverly, her best friend. They were on their way to the river. Mayjean had a washer and dryer in the house; all their laundry was done at home now. Modern conveniences had come to Chantilly, but some folks still used the river for washing and bathing. McKenna enjoyed the river; she was always drawn to the roar of the rushing water. Most of the village women had already gone to the river today; Saturday was always washday.

A smiling, plump Beverly came up the road. She waved to Mayjean as McKenna came down to meet her. The friends had been together since elementary school. Beverly was the shorter of the two. Fairly attractive, witty, and dependable, she had defended McKenna many times. McKenna's more slender willowy figure was a sharp contrast to Beverly's robust and wider curves. McKenna could tell her best friend her innermost thoughts without being judged. The young women had lived fairly similar lifestyles, although McKenna had grown up more sheltered. Beverly had experienced puberty way before her friend. McKenna had seen breasts spout almost overnight on her friend and wondered if the same would ever happen to her. When McKenna's period came at fourteen, she carried around the secret for two whole days before she told anyone. She had been deathly afraid that she had contracted a disease and was about to die. Beverly had experienced boyfriends and sex, unlike McKenna.

Rey, one of the village musicians, always teased the girls.

"Belle Jolie, beautiful ladies, take me along with you today, I beg you." "I will be very good."

"You don't know how to be good." The young women laughed.

Rey replied, "Ah! You wound me." "You girls never give me a chance."

Rey had spent some time in one of the French Islands. He was a good sort, but he had an eye for the ladies. He played in the village band every year for Carnival. His songs were a mixture of the island soca and his own flamboyant personality. He was in the process of setting up the band for the upcoming carnival celebration.

On their long walk to the riverbank, the friends caught up on the past days' events. McKenna's anger with Mayjean came out in a rush. "You know, Bev, I've been the best granddaughter she could ask for." "I have never made any trouble." "I just want to live my life." "She won't let me." "I mean, I'm twenty years old, for crying out loud." "This is ridiculous." "She keeps saying that Chantilly is not in my future."

Suddenly McKenna's dream popped into her consciousness. She had never told Beverly about her dreams. McKenna had a sudden premonition that maybe Mayjean was right, but she wasn't ready to admit to it.

"So what brought all this on?" asked Beverly.

"Well, I've been speaking to Brian a while now."

"Are you dating him?" "No!" It's complicated. Brian broke up a while now with his last girlfriend. I kind of helped him get over it. We spent a lot of time talking. Now he wants to be with me."

"Do you want to be with him?"

"Truthfully, I don't know. I have never been with a man, not in the real sense anyways. I think I'm tempted. He's not a bad guy, although Mayjean doesn't think so. I mean, he has a job, his own place—well, his parents' place. They live overseas. They won't be back here anytime soon."

"Have you kissed him?"

"Yes, I have. It was just okay, nothing special."

"How would you know since you haven't done it before?"

"Well, I expected to feel excited, tingly, or something. I felt nothing."

The friends shared a conspiratorial smile.

"Well, you should follow your heart and take it slowly," said a brightly smiling Beverly.

Upon reaching the riverbank, they found their favorite spot. At a bend in the river, a massive tree had fallen during a hurricane, years before the friends were girls. They had played so many times on this tree. While eating the lunch they had brought, their legs would dangle in the cool refreshing water flowing beneath. They giggled like schoolgirls as they remembered yesterday. The passage of time had already left indelible marks on their psyche, and they were not even full-fledged adults.

The innocence of childhood beckoned in that unguarded moment. Adulthood, with all its resulting responsibilities, burdens, and problems, could wait a little while longer. The riverbed was alive with life. In the clear water, little crabs and other shellfish burrowed further into the mud. Small mullet fish darted to and fro, at times coming close to the surface in search of food crumbs. At the water's edge, huge trees shooting up to the sky vied for sunlight and space. All of nature was in harmony; even the tiny water grass and ferns nestled in the roots of the trees and on low-lying rocks seemed content. The lush greenery contrasted with the monotonous ebb and flow of the currents, creating a relaxing atmosphere. The occasional cry of waterfowl and other birds were the only other sounds intruding upon this idyllic place. This was paradise. Everything in nature was innocent yet knowledgeable, seemingly unmarked but buffeted by currents and time. Even the smooth pebbles underfoot spoke a language more eloquent than speech itself.

The day with Beverly had been a boon to McKenna's spirit. She had come back feeling energized and full of purpose. Mayjean had noticed the difference instantly. A little bit at a time, the women's relationship improved. They wore matching smiles of contentment and peace. An ease inhabited the Samuel household once more, and they shared in some village humor. Someone in Chantilly always made a spectacle of themselves. Like today, one of the gossips, Yvonne, had gotten her story wrong. She had accused Tin—tin, a village ruffian, of stealing coconuts off the Serrants' land. Tin-tin had cursed her in every which way. The villagers had a field day when it was found out that Tin-tin had worked for the Serrants and the coconuts were part of his compensation. Yvonne had been standing on the streets when the news broke. She had to take a long walk of shame to her home, with the accompaniment of people jeering and laughing at her. She never lifted her head again until she was out of sight.

Mayjean's fish broth was long overdue. McKenna was given the task of grating the coconut; its milk was integral to the *sancoche* dish. The biggest pot in the house was bubbling with the banana, plantains, and yams cooking in salted water. The fish had been scaled and gutted; they now sat in a marinade of lime, salt, and pepper, waiting to join the medley in the pot. Mayjean always cooked extra food. Her mother had always said it was better to have too much food if a visitor came by than not to have enough. The smell of Mayjean's cooking always drew someone to their door. Sure enough, Christina and her whole house came just as the pot was coming off the fire.

As they sat down to eat, Christina blessed the food. Mayjean couldn't help remarking how good her daughter looked. Christina's skin shone with health and vitality. The bump of her pregnancy was more noticeable now. She looked happy and well rested; she beamed with an inner light.

"Since I came from the hospital, I have been going to that Christian church now, and I gave my heart to Jesus."

Mayjean sat up straighter in her chair; she was listening to Christina with her undivided attention. When she heard "I am getting married," her fork fell from fingers suddenly numb with shock.

After Mayjean recovered, she started crying. Things were starting to turn around for Christina.

"So who is this man?" asked a tearful Mayjean, overcome with emotion. "His name is Mark, the same drifter you were talking about. We have decided to live our lives for Christ. He has been very good to me. I finally found the one, Mom. I wanted to tell you first before I brought him over. Do I have your blessing, Mayjean?"

"Of course, my child. Mi never thought mi'd see the day. I am very happy for you."

"You see, it's never too late," said Christina.

"Well, nuh fu me, nuh. Mi done wid men," said Mayjean. "Mi have McKenna to take care of."

"McKenna can take care of herself. She's no longer a child. She's an adult," said a proud Christina, glancing her daughter's way.

McKenna went over and gave her mom a heartfelt hug.

"Congratulations, Christina." She had never called her mom before, and she wouldn't start now. Mayjean would always be her mom.

Christina's visit lasted far into the night. Mayjean and Christina were slowly mending their fractured relationship. It was amazing what good news could do to boost morale. At least there were no fights this time around. The get-togethers were not always peaceful.

When the house was again empty, Mayjean took out her leaves.

"You had that dream again."

"Yes, Mamajean. It becomes more vivid each time. I can't explain why."

"Don't worry, my child. I give yu something. You'll sleep peaceful tonight."

McKenna gave the only mother she knew a big hug and took the tea. She was asleep before her head hit the pillow.

Chapter 5

Chantilly's charm was in its people. McKenna knew almost everyone by name. People were generally kind and friendly unless you upset them. The drawback to living in such a small community was that everyone was always in everyone else's affairs. Gossip spread like wildfire in Chantilly. At work, some women had gathered outside the credit union. She overheard them calling her name. One of the nosy buddies was actually brave enough to confront her, saying, "You daye wid Brian." McKenna laughed it off; sometimes it was better to remain silent than to give people more ammunition. They would soon move on to the next item.

On her lunch break, some of the young men in the village had picked up the story and started calling her names connecting her to Brian. McKenna's day became unbearable; she started getting angry. If only the story was true. Her head felt heavy; she couldn't wait to get home. Margery, the manager, noticed how flushed and uncomfortable she seemed. Her entreaties of "are you all right" were met with a sullen "I'm fine, thank you."

McKenna realized someone was fueling the grapevine. She would have to see Brian this evening to iron this out. She hated lying to Mayjean. She would have to go when Mayjean fell asleep. This couldn't wait. By the time she got home, she had a nasty headache. Mayjean took one look at her and gave her the same tea as before. She never saw Brian that night. Trouble had slipped in unnoticed like a thief in the night and had caught her unawares and unprepared. The good reputation that Mayjean had said all women should have seemed poised to flee and leave McKenna in ruins.

If something happened in Chantilly, odds were Mayjean knew about it or she would soon find out. She got the news that trouble was underfoot. Anything that concerned McKenna bothered Mayjean too. Mayjean's spies had already notified her of the perpetrator spreading the vicious lies. Mayjean prepared for battle. She said her prayers and went for a bath at her special place. Invigorated and clear headed, she made her way to the bottom end of the village.

This part of Chantilly had never been fully built up, compared to the rest of the village. Many governmental projects that had begun to improve the area always ended when a new political party took office. In the heyday of the banana boom, when the Caribbean had enjoyed preferential treatment from Britain for their bananas, the villagers themselves had built up some newer structures. With the economy now in disarray, some of the homes were now broken down and falling apart.

Mayjean walked to a row of small dilapidated homes.

"Marlene . . . it's me—Mayjean. How you do? Hold di dog. Mi nuh want im bite mi."

"Ah wah go an. Lang time mi nuh see yu," said a smiling, gap-toothed Marlene. The dog was barking viciously, creating a loud din. "Come inside. It's quieter. The old foot bothering me man."

After they explained pleasantries, Mayjean asked where Beverly was.

"Oh, I don't know. Things haven't been good with us lately. She too flighty for me. Every minute she has a new man. She hangs around the wrong crowd in the city. I tired tell her mom to send for that girl. My health ain't as it used to be. I ain't strong no more, or I would show her who is de boss. The youths of today too difficult to manage, yu hear. Mi just want peace. Since my Rufus gone, things have changed round here. Her brother is the obedient one. He gets good grades and is always studying. He says he wants to be a lawyer."

"Beverly has changed a lot. She spent some time wid McKenna the other day," said Mayjean in a calm voice. "Now mi hearing a story she is spreading, telling people McKenna wid Brian. I want to know which Brian. I don't want him. My daughter deserves better. She too good for that runaround."

"True? She say dat? No! She wouldn't do that. She loves McKenna. They have been good girls together," said a distraught Marlene. "Yu sure?" replied Marlene. "I can't believe she would do that."

The dog started up his barking again, and in walked Beverly. When she saw Mayjean, she pulled up short, and fear registered on her face. Mayjean gave her no time before she pounced.

"You know why I'm here, don't you?"

"What are you talking about?"

"Oh, girlie, you know."

Beverly held Mayjean's stare for all of ten seconds, and then she caved in.

"I'm so sorry, Mayjean. I never meant to harm McKenna. It was a stupid mistake. It won't happen again."

"You better tell your friends then to stop dragging my daughter's name through the mud!" Mayjean was hopping mad now, and her eyes were shooting daggers at a shaking Beverly. "Yu don't want to see my face here again."

"Yes, Mamajean, I'm sorry."

Mayjean said her good-byes to Marlene and left Beverly to deal with her grandmother's wrath.

McKenna's first brush with real betrayal; was like a bitter brew, the aftertaste acrid. She never thought Beverly had it in her to hurt her like that. She had noticed small changes in her friend over the years. She seemed angry, not the carefree girl she used to know. She had always lived vicariously through Beverly escapades; she now realized there was a price to pay for that knowledge. Beverly had been hurt by other people and didn't think twice now about hurting others. She would forgive her, but their friendship had been irretrievably damaged. How could one continue to be friends with someone they couldn't trust? She had known Beverly all of her life. This really hurt; it more than sucked. Mayjean did her best to console her grieving daughter. She made McKenna's favorite foods and shared some of her own life stories. Over the next couple of days, they passed the time crocheting and chatting, especially in the evenings, when McKenna came home.

When McKenna finally caught up with Brian, he was quite pleased with the situation. His pretend indifference was written all over his smirking face. Brian felt his chances were becoming better with the scandal. He was glad McKenna's name had been linked to his. To most young men in the village, she was a catch in more ways than one. At twenty, McKenna was still innocent of men; the village males all wanted to be the one. It would never happen if Mayjean had her way. Mayjean knew McKenna was destined for greatness, and like a mother hen, she had kept a watchful eye over her all these years.

Some people like to hold on to grudges. It gives them something to be angry at. Resentment toward the two Samuel women had been building steadily for sometime now. When a kettle boils, the steam only escapes in intermittent bursts, so to the scandal was the primer. More was to follow; the tide had turned against the two women. The first salvo paved the way for the rest of the deluge. People had always whispered that Mayjean was a witch. Now the gossips said that McKenna was being trained in obeah too. Every mistake Mayjean had made in the past was twice magnified. Beulah, one of the village gossips, said within Mayjean's hearing, "Who does she think she is, nuh? "Anthony nuh mi want she . . . chups." The older woman took it all in stride. She knew better than to argue with Beulah; it wasn't worth it.

The young men had been angry at McKenna's refusal to date them. The sentiment that ran in the village was that Mayjean and her daughter felt that they were too good for Chantilly. Some people felt that Mayjean had no right to accost Beverly. Lines were drawn and sides chosen: camp Beverly versus McKenna. Differences always scared people; McKenna's uncommon beauty had caused jealousy for some time now. The scandal had created an outlet for the villagers' anger and resentment. McKenna's bronzed but paler skin, long hair, and defined bone structure created quite a contrast in Chantilly. Her difference was exotic; the fascination with the young woman at times bordered on rudeness.

Mayjean had always been comfortable with her nature. She knew secret things others didn't know. No two people are the same; each individual is a unique blueprint filled with purpose. Messages came to her on the wind. She considered herself fortunate to be blessed with such gifts. Her difference threatened others. When people needed her help, they were happy for her gifts then. Only this morning, a woman she had helped during childbirth when her baby had been breached passed by without so much as a hello and had the nerve to cross her eyes. Mayjean had called out to her; she then responded with a quick "how you do" and scurried into a grocery shop. Mayjean would confess to reading the Bible, but evil she had never done. They could talk all they wanted. If she was of the devil, they wouldn't be saying it. How they were not afraid of her evil, she couldn't fathom that one. They would soon come knocking at her door, give them time; they always did. Her only fear was for her daughter. McKenna didn't even know she had natural talent hidden within her. Christina had never bothered with honing her skills, and she was too busy raising child after child. The Samuel women were born natural healers.

McKenna sat playing the piano. Her head bent in concentration, she was oblivious to her surroundings. Her long hair fell in a halo, hiding her spectacular beauty. McKenna's beauty drew heads everywhere she went. Men would sometimes stop and stare at the young woman. She was never vain but unaware of her effect on the opposite sex. The Serrant part of her heritage was becoming more apparent in the tinge of her skin and lush features. Her grandfather Anthony had gotten the piano as a gift for her birthday many years ago.

The soft music beguiled Mayjean's senses. She closed her eyes in surrender and listened with pride as McKenna played. Music transported her. All her cares seemed to magically float away, and she existed in a state of euphoria. Music was a peculiar pleasure, a godsend. Mayjean could play a little, but she enjoyed listening to the younger woman play. McKenna would make a great wife and mother one day. The spirits had told Mayjean that a great man would marry her daughter; the news had come to her a long time ago. She reflected on the last couple of weeks. Some of the villagers had been hard on them. People had made up all sorts of stories. Unshakeable faith in God had seen them through. Mayjean knew nothing about obeah, but she knew how to pray and follow the leadings of the Holy Spirit.

Eventually the scandal blew over, and McKenna emerged stronger and more radiant than ever. She was happy to be in other people's company again. Brian had taken a backseat in her life for now. She had met Beverly after work one day in the streets. It was very awkward at first to say, hello but the other woman had apologized. Christina's wedding was coming up, and McKenna was very busy helping. For the first time in her life, she was getting to know the woman who had birthed her. Christina was actually a lot of fun. Like a flower slowly unfurling in the sunlight, their tenuous bond was becoming stronger.

Chapter 6

The village bus from Chantilly hugged the serpentine curves of a bumpy road as it sped on its way into the city. Inside the vehicle, the jerky motion jostled passengers and bags alike. McKenna always grabbed a window seat. As a child, she had been prone to bouts of motion sickness and nausea, which had often resulted in vomiting. Today Mayjean made the trip with her. Mayjean was coming to stock up on provisions, and McKenna was going to the big library.

They had left the village on the earliest bus, which always left at five thirty in the morning. At this time of day, the dawn was fast approaching. It was a very peaceful time. All of nature was just coming awake. The village roosters were creating quite a ruckus; crows of cock a doodle were repeated many times, alerting the universe that a new day had arrived. Some people were still abed, but others had started the trek to their garden plots in the hills. Alvin, the bus driver, was a rotund jolly fellow. He knew his way in and around the whole island of Belantine. Today his wife and daughter sat up front, enjoying the view but also glad they were not being squeezed like the other passengers.

McKenna had often traveled up front. She had spent two years being bused every day when she went to the community college in the city. The buses in the islands were not built for comfort. They were the means of transport to get people and goods from one location to another. On Fridays, most villagers went to the city; the bus was filled to capacity. Alvin was a

Christian believer, and at this time of the morning, his radio played gospel favorites as people sat in silence, still sleeping from waking so early. 'The Grace Thrillers' song "Can't Even Walk" was on at the moment. The song had been played so many times in Mayjean's home that McKenna knew all the words. She looked out on the passing scenery to see the darkness finally receding.

The sun's rays were just coming up over the crest of the mountains, and they reflected off the glass of the bus. A day like today was her favorite kind of day; sometimes one just knew deep in their bones that a day was special. She never failed to appreciate the beauty of her homeland. An abundant green carpet of dense forest covered the road on both sides. They had left the sleepy little villages behind about an hour ago. The roads wound through the mountains before descending into the city. The mountains were truly beautiful; lush flora and fauna abounded here. Interspersed among the vivid green trees, vines, and shrubs were wild flowers of every shape and size. McKenna had always felt this is what the garden of Eden must have looked like.

All too soon, the city loomed outside the window. Mayjean had fallen asleep on herself. McKenna nudged her awake. The bus had also come to life; people were wide awake. They were giving Alvin instructions on where they should be dropped of. The trip into the city always began with a swanky breakfast in a nice restaurant. Mayjean picked Tilda's. They had been there many times before. People were milling about inside. The restaurant was housed in a building dominated by French architecture from the colonial era. Spacious and high ceilinged, the style was designed for the warm Caribbean climate. The day was beginning to get warm, but a cool morning wind lingered indoors.

Some noisy Caucasian tourists on vacation were enjoying the authentic Caribbean cuisine. Mayjean and McKenna were seated at a table on a porch overlooking the street, and off to the side, another part of the city lay in the distance. The wide-hipped roof extended over the patio, creating intimacy and providing shade. McKenna always broke her fast with fresh fruit. She asked the waiter for a fruit platter. He returned with a dish lined with slivers of sweet mangoes, papayas, melons, oranges, and bananas lovingly displayed to perfection. The design was almost too beautiful to eat. Mayjean ordered tea, liver stew on a bed of lettuce, and fresh-baked bread. The outside patio was separated by a set of small French doors. An inquisitive, chubby, bright-eyed girl of about three played hide-and-seek with McKenna from behind the many small panes of glass.

After eating, the women planned what they would do next. Mayjean wanted to go to the market first, so they agreed to meet in an hour's time.

McKenna took her time enjoying the sight and sounds of the city. Vehicles honked as they jockeyed for position in the busy streets. People wove in and out of traffic carrying shopping bags while some held on to their children's arms. She passed vendors selling their wares. Some were quietly sitting in booths while the more enterprising would loudly and boldly shout out their offerings. A group of young men sat idly around a corner. A game of dominoes was being played in the group. Unemployment was always an issue; it was felt acutely in the city. Unlike in the village, one could always get by with a handout or some food from a neighbor's tree. In the city, if you didn't have, you either starved or contribute to the growing crime rate. Sometimes she daydreamed about being rich enough to make a difference; life wasn't always easy.

Going up the library steps, a shy young man smiled at her. McKenna smiled back. "How are you doing?" she asked. "Good! You?" he replied. Her mood was expansive. The city was a nice contrast from Chantilly. In the city, no one knew your name. She liked the anonymity and the freedom she found here.

The library was located in a quiet older part of the city. The building was a three-story unit painted in a subdued black and white with red trim. McKenna knew the layout like the back of her hand. She had spent countless hours within these walls researching and studying her school materials. Her college friends had preferred partying and fun to their books. McKenna had excelled in her studies and had many awards to show for it. Now she came mostly for her own reading pleasure. Life without books would be like living in an airless prison. The seeker in McKenna needed the challenge of pleasure and knowledge found in reading. It wasn't enough just to know; the path of wisdom lay in the questioning.

The hour was up before she had a chance to select her books. McKenna quickly grabbed a few she had been perusing and rushed to meet the older woman. The sun was high in the sky, and the mercury was steadily rising when she arrived at the square. In the heat, the cacophony of many voices assailed her immediately. The smell of the ripe and colorful array of produce included plantains, bananas, passion fruit, limes, and mangoes; this scene was a familiar one. They had made this trip at least once a month, as far back as McKenna could remember. The market was always a lively and colorful place. The hot weather did not deter the islanders; living in the tropics, the heat was a constant companion. Fresh produce and other food delicacies were being battered everywhere.

Consumers here were very knowledgeable about prices and were busy hopping from one stall to the next. The market was divided into sections: the produce and fruit stalls were up at the very front while the fish-and-meat mongers stood toward the back of the square. Mayjean always knew which vendors had the best produce. Mayjean and McKenna had agreed to meet at Rocco's stall. Mayjean had befriended the woman years ago.

"McKenna, chile, how you doing?" Rocco gave McKenna a warm hug. It was always good to see Rocco. "You all grown up, McKenna."

"Yes," said Mayjean.

"The girl will marry soon."

"In due time," replied Mayjean.

After they had talked about some other city gossip, the women bid Rocco good-bye. They went to their favorite grocer and bought wholesale goods. Alvin collected their packages, which freed them up for lunch. Mayjean had to see her doctor before they left the city. McKenna had noticed that her grandmother seemed tired more often lately. She had asked Mayjean if she was well. Mayjean had replied "never better," so McKenna had not pressed the issue further. Mayjean could be a stubborn woman when she wanted to be.

The city was a melting pot of many cultures. The influences of the British, French, West African, and indigenous peoples that had shaped the Caribbean could be seen everywhere. Evidence could be found in the rich architecture, diverse dishes, and the multiple languages spoken so eloquently. The faces in the city were all different yet similar; the heritage of the Caribbean stamped indelibly in everyone.

Mayjean had gone into a little out-of-the way store tucked at the entrance to an alleyway in the heart of the downtown. McKenna browsed outside while she waited. Her back was turned to the street as she looked at a colorful skirt swaying in the breeze outside the shop.

"Dinah! Dinah!" The voice was insistent. A short brown-skinned man, a straw hat covering his head, hurried up to McKenna. In his hands he carried two plastic bags, "Dinah, didn't you . . . Oh! I'm sorry. Excuse me, miss. Forgive me, I took you for someone else." He backed away in confusion. That was a strange occurrence, thought McKenna.

At lunchtime, the women found a small family diner and ordered two plates of *pelau*, a Caribbean dish of rice stewed with vegetables and chicken. Enjoying the hot, mildly spiced meal, McKenna looked up to find a pair of black hard eyes trained on her. A young black man in his mid—to late twenties sat alone, polishing a similar plate of food. His companion was a tall glass of yellow passion fruit juice, frothy and delectable with chinks of ice swirling at the top. He was smiling almost imperceptibly at McKenna. She thought two could play at this game. She totally ignored him and struck up a conversation with Mayjean. She was telling Mayjean of the strange little man, his accent, and the mistaken identity. This was an eventful day for sure.

Across from her, the stranger's hot stare burned her face. The man shifted in his seat so he could focus all of his attention on her. He was appealing in an obvious sort of way; he was on the prowl. She found herself comparing him to Brian. Brian was the more attractive of the two. He wasn't handsome, not in the traditional sense, but his appeal was in his boldness. She didn't understand why, but she was intrigued. It felt as if he was committing each little detail of her face to memory. She gave him a genuine smile and saw how he lapped it up. They were two strangers sharing a smile over lunch; a little flirting never harmed no one. Mayjean pretended innocence; the girl was allowed to have some fun. The young man waved to McKenna as he left, a big grin on his cheeky face.

Their last stop of the day was at Mayjean's doctor. McKenna waited while Mayjean went in. When Mayjean came out after about forty minutes, McKenna was quite concerned. A gray pallor now rested on her previously relaxed countenance. She seemed shaken and out of sorts, and her brown eyes wouldn't meet McKenna's.

"Mamajean, are you okay? What's wrong? You don't look so well. Should I speak to Dr. Russ?"

"It's nothing, chile, nothing a little rest won't cure. Don't get worried. Everything okay. Let's go home."

They made their way to the bus depot. Everyone was waiting and ready to go back home. The return trip was always uncomfortable. Groceries and packages were shoved into every available space; some of the bags rested in the laps of the owners.

The villagers were tired but happy with their purchases. Alvin's bus was full of chatter as people recounted the many experiences and deals that were found that day. The city was full of excitement, but familiar comforts beckoned weary travelers home. McKenna was quite happy with her books; she had started reading one at the doctor's office. The encounter with the man in the diner today had her thinking of Brian. She wanted to see him again. She was glad Mayjean was caught up in the conversations going on around them. McKenna was lost in her own daydreams.

Chapter 7

McKenna had achieved the pinnacle of education on Belantine. She had stayed in Chantilly to be with her aging grandmother; Christina had never figured into her plans. She could have found a better job in the city, but Mayjean would not hear of it. McKenna had even suggested they move there together, but Mayjean could not be persuaded. McKenna was ready to spread her wings. Eventually she wanted her own family, a husband, and a couple of children. She had other dreams she wanted to fulfill though. She wanted to be somebody, to do something meaningful with her life. Her Aunt Ruby lived in Canada; she had invited McKenna to come for a vacation many times. McKenna had thought about moving to live with Ruby and her family. Ruby had two girls; one was of McKenna's age. They had corresponded over the years growing up.

She felt terrible leaving Mayjean behind; guilt would assail her every time she thought about it. The woman was set in her ways; she didn't want to travel overseas now. McKenna yearned to travel and to explore the world. She wanted to be an active participant in her own life. Even now she was aware that there was something more that awaited her, something bigger than herself.

Learning fascinated her. At eighteen, she had finished community college. These past two years, she worked as a teller in the small credit union. The services were mainly geared toward the people of the community. People would deposit their hard-earned money in the village bank instead of travelling to the city. When they needed cash, it was readily available. The surplus revenue generated went into community projects the villagers voted on. However, tourists and others passing through benefited from the service; they would most often need to convert their money or get additional information. McKenna was getting tired of waiting though; this waiting, this delayed expectation was now wearing on her nerves. She had read so much about other cultures; she had a yearning to experience the old Mayan ruins, to visit Paris and walk its romantic streets. McKenna daydreamed about the English countryside. Reading William Shakespeare was not enough; she wanted to see it through her own eyes.

Mayjean had complained about being tired earlier in the afternoon. She had taken one of the pills Dr. Russ had given her. She was in a deep sleep, and McKenna thought she would take a walk, maybe visit Brian and see what he was up to. Her knock on his door revealed a smiling Brian.

"What is the occasion, princess?" replied a happy and grinning Brian.

"Thought I'd come say hello. Too early to sleep."

"Well, come in then. I'm all alone. So how have you been? I missed you," replied Brian.

"You know where I live, you know. Afraid of Mayjean," said a breathy McKenna.

"Me? No! Why should I be?"

"You know why," replied McKenna. "Mayjean is sleeping. That's why I came."

"You look very beautiful this evening." McKenna was wearing casual blue jeans and a simple black tank. Her hair lay unbraided and flowing down her back.

"You flatterer, it's the same me. Nothing's changed. I'm not even dressed up," said McKenna, moving around the dining area.

"You are still beautiful to me. Every time I see you, you take my breath away," Brian was staring intently at McKenna.

To break up the intense mood, McKenna interjected "are you going to show me around."

McKenna had always spoken to Brian outside his house. She had glimpses of his home, but she had never ventured inside until to tonight. She had entered the den of the lion. If she had any sense in her head, she would have run by now. She shouldn't have been in his home alone with him. He seemed nice, but there was something about him that was off.

Brian was about six feet tall. He had a trim physique like most of the young men on the island. She liked his height. He was a good-looking male specimen, and he knew it. She wasn't as attracted to him as she thought she would have been. Women always knew these things. There was something about him that kept her on edge.

Brian was saying, "This house has been in my family for over fifty years." It had started out smaller, but over the years, they had added to it. He was born within the walls. His parents had five children, four were overseas. He was the black sheep of the family, and he liked being a loner. That McKenna had in common with him.

Brian was only a couple of years older than she was, but he had already lived a lifetime. His home was very nice, sparely furnished, and very male. As far as the eye could see, nothing frilly or any soft touches reminiscent of femininity could be found. Instead, straight lines and hard edges dominated.

They settled in his black couch to chat.

"So, McKenna, tell me what do you want out of life," said Brian.

McKenna replied, "I want many things, I feel many things. It's difficult to explain."

"Most women I know just want a husband and children," explained Brain. "You are a complicated woman. I like easy. Life is difficult enough," replied Brian.

"You asked, I told you," McKenna was a little annoyed. Most men felt that a women's place was in the home and raising children. She wanted that too, but there would be more for her; no one would tell her otherwise.

The whole time they were talking, Brian's hand had slowly crept along her thigh. She left it there for now. Brian was trying to charm her; she had come fully knowing she was going to kiss him. After tonight, she would know if she would continue with him.

Brian worked in the small island airport, and he drove his own vehicle. He had a carefree attitude toward life. When they had talked over the last little while, he had come across as a more caring person. Now she wasn't so sure. In his pain, he had reached out to her, but the charmer in him was back.

His hands suddenly grabbed both of hers. She looked up at him. His face blocked out the light, and his head descended. She did not evade him. His kiss was rough and desperate. McKenna allowed it, and she sat unmoving. After a couple of moments, he became gentler and tried to coax her. She was unsure and plain confused. She felt nothing. She had enough though. Her hands moved to stop him. Brian pushed her hands down and tried to force her deeper into the couch. McKenna knew fear. She realized now she should have listened to that little voice inside her. This was not what she wanted. Her efforts to push him off her met with stubborn resistance.

"Stop," she pleaded. "I don't want this."

"Why did you come here then?"

"I don't know . . . To talk to someone, to have some company." She now realized that Brian was the wrong guy.

"You want me. Come on, you know you do," said an incredulous Brian. The idea that McKenna was different and she didn't want him hadn't sunk into his brain yet. He was selfishly thinking about himself. It was always about Brian.

"Get off me . . . right now!" McKenna was angry. She was no match for his enormous strength. She started struggling in earnest as Brian pinned her hands by her side and started kissing her neck.

"Please stop, I beg you. Don't do this. Brian, please stop! . . . God . . . no, please!"

Brian was past caring.

In her home, Mayjean lay dreaming. In the vision, she saw McKenna struggling with a man. She knew instinctively it was Brian and that he was trying to rape her daughter. Mayjean tried to wake from her sleep, but the pills she had taken had knocked her out. She tried valiantly to rise. Helpless and immobile, the tears rolled down her face. In the vision, McKenna was screaming

"No! Please stop." Mayjean sent strength vibrations to McKenna. Brian had better run. After this, there would be nowhere he could hide where she would not find him. The drugged sleep caught Mayjean again, and she succumbed. Her bond with her granddaughter was so strong she sometimes got visions of the girl when she was in danger.

McKenna felt a surge of power, and she started bucking Brian off her body. She created enough momentum to get one hand released. It was that hand that clawed at his face. One of her nails had found some soft skin; he relinquished his hold to grab at his face. She bolted off his couch and never looked back as she ran without her shoes for the sanctuary of her home. She had narrowly missed being assaulted. She locked and bolted her door and added a chair for extra security. Adrenaline kicked in, and she started to shake. It was an uncontrollable bone-rattling shaking that wouldn't stop. A deep coldness permeated every inch of her body. McKenna realized she was going into shock; her favorite blanket could not warm her. Her teeth wouldn't stop chattering. She grabbed some more blankets, and eventually some warmth seeped back into her chilled frame. She was feeling more like herself again. If Mayjean found out, it would not be pretty.

Suddenly Mayjean was there. She went into the kitchen, and in no time, a cup was placed in McKenna's hand. "Drink this, daughter." This time the brew was more pungent; a strong smell of the leaves and spices Mayjean had used wafted up to her nostrils. "It will help you forget. Come and lie in my bed." McKenna did not understand how her grandmother knew. It was years since she had slept in her grandmother's bed. She was very grateful for Mayjean's body warmth and physical presence right now. After the young woman had drifted off, Mayjean looked at her daughter. There would be trouble on the morrow; someone would be leaving the village, and it wouldn't be them.

It was still early when Mayjean left home. She made sure McKenna was still asleep. The tea she had given her was a healing concoction that would help her forget her ordeal. Mayjean herself had drunk it many times. McKenna would fight her own battles, but today Brian needed to hear a few home truths. He always left for work early so she wanted to accost him before it turned seven o'clock. He would not get anytime to spin his lies down at the village shop. Like vultures, they were always circling and waiting for any chance of weakness to pounce on unsuspecting young girls.

Brian had an inkling that the older woman would surface, but he was taken aback to see her so early in the morning. He recovered quickly and tried to close his door.

"You better open di door." Mayjean wasn't above a little blackmail. "Mi make such a noise, bwoye, everybody come."

Brian was embarrassed by what he had done, and he didn't want his perfidy known. He opened that door so quick, it was like he was on fire and he needed saving. Mayjean was understandably upset.

"My heart is grieved by how you treated McKenna. How could you?" said an agitated Mayjean as she went nose to nose with Brian. "Why you'd want to hurt her. She said to stop, I heard her."

Brian's head went up.

"You heard what! Old woman, you were in your bed. McKenna is my woman," said a gloating Brian.

"No, she is not." This time Mayjean was shaking with her anger. "She is not yours, and she never will be! You hear me! Lousy good for nuthing, you better get it in your head."

"Or what?" replied Brian. "You going to obeah me!"

"Me? I don't know nuthing about your obeah," said Mayjean. "My God is more powerful than any obeah, yu hear. Yu better start running! If yu touch my daughter again, yu will see another side of me yu don't want to see." Mayjean couldn't believe the nerve of Brian. "McKenna don't want yu. Yu have nothing she wants!" Mayjean stamped her foot in anger. "Brian, try me! Yu think I joking, eh! My daughter too good for yu." Mayjean's parting shot was "McKenna is a woman of substance. Something yu will never know about."

That night had changed McKenna. Now she stayed far away from Brian and most of the village men. She had retreated into her self; her books were always a source of comfort. The last two betrayals had hit her hard. Her spirit wasn't broken and defeated, but she was shell-shocked to say the least. Mayjean had started teaching her about the native plants and showed her how to make the teas and poultices. McKenna took notes and compiled them in a big box she placed high on a shelf in her room. Some folks in Chantilly were aware of some of what had happened between Brian and McKenna. Though no one spoke openly about the affair, whispers could be heard in little groups when Mayjean and McKenna walked in the streets. Brian had taken Mayjean's threats to heart. Some weeks later, he had packed up his bags and moved to the city. McKenna had breathed a huge sigh of relief. It had been difficult and embarrassing running into him; Chantilly was too small of a place to avoid him.

McKenna had learned some valuable lessons. She had resolved to always listen to that inner voice. She had known deep down that Brian was not the man for her. She would be more careful next time in her choices. Mayjean had always been there, but she knew there would come a time when she had to rely on her own ingenuity. Though she hadn't met him yet, she knew the man of her dreams would be a seeker, someone attractive, of course. A man who was dependable, trustworthy, a man of integrity, someone she could grow old with. She knew it would happen, eventually. Male and female needed each other; it was predestined.

Chapter 8

Preparations for Christina's wedding were in full swing. Christina had blown her budget. Mayjean gave her some of the money she had being saving over the years to help her out. Mark, Christina's soon-to-be-husband, seemed a good sort. McKenna thought him quite brave to take on Christina and all her baggage. They were to be married on the following Saturday. Christina wanted it to be official before the baby came. Mayjean was pleased as punch; she had welcomed Mark into the family with open arms.

Mayjean realized her time with her family was short. She didn't want to scare or worry them, so she had kept her illness to herself. McKenna was quite capable of taking care of herself now; Mayjean had taught her everything she knew. The younger woman had a good head on her shoulders. Everything was coming together nicely. Mayjean actually smiled through a sudden jolt of small tremors. The pain was more pronounced these days. She didn't know what she would have done without Dr. Russ. The pills he had given helped tremendously. Before the sharp edged pain would have made her double over; now it was a dull throb. She would hold on though until that man that was promised would come for her daughter. She willed it to happen soon.

In the village, excitement had sprung up over Christina's big day. Some of the other unmarried women were jealous, while others said she deserved it and her time had come. When Saturday rolled around, not a cloud was in the sky. It was as if

God himself had ordained the day. The caterers spent all day preparing the wedding feast. In the afternoon, a crowd gathered outside the little Methodist church to watch the proceedings. After the bridegroom had entered and sat in the church for a while, the little procession of bride and bridesmaids followed. Christina's daughters were attired in bright fuchsia, and McKenna led the pack. Christina wore a wide radiant smile, her pregnancy concealed in the yards of white fabric that was her dress.

Mayjean rounded up the procession decked out in her finest ensemble to date. Her daughter Ruby, who lived in Canada, had sent a red and white silk dress for the occasion, which fitted impeccably. Her white hat sat on her head at a steep angle. In her high heels, she walked like a regal queen. There were cheers and catcalls as Mayjean went into the church. Her smiles of joy were palpable. The wedding party consisted of distant family and mostly close friends from Chantilly and the surrounding villages. After the vows were said, the newly married couple walked out of the church amid more cheers and loud hand claps. The reception took place in one of the two halls in the village.

McKenna had a blast. It wasn't every day a Samuel got married. She saw herself getting married but under different circumstances. The party went far into the night, as most villagers always welcomed any opportunity to let loose. Well-wishers joined the merriment, and a good time was had by all. Mayjean had left the young ones to their fun; she needed her rest. McKenna reflected on the failures her mother and Mayjean had in their past relationships. She would be heartbroken if that happened to her.

It was some months since things had quieted down in Chantilly. The summer months were upon Belantine, and people were out and about enjoying the beaches and nature's bounty. Mangoes and other fruit were ripening under the heat of the hot sun. Children, home from school, would roam far and wide. Their mothers' call sometimes would be met with silence because they had already flown the coop.

McKenna spent long days lazing away on a beach or frolicking in a river under bright sunny skies. She had almost forgotten about Brian's vileness. Though guarded, she allowed herself to have some fun. She wanted to trust people again. Grace and her other siblings would take her along on their trips. As a child, she had been closeted. This new freedom to do as she pleased went to her head like strong wine. Their forays into the bush yielded *pwadus*, a pod of pea like delicacies that melted with sweetness on the tongue.

The bush also nestled bugs and ants of every variety. One day she had stood unawares in a nest of red ants. By the time she had become aware of their existence, they had crawled up her legs and were making a meal of her thighs. Her shrieks alerted the others to her distress. They started laughing and led her into the nearby river to cool her burning legs. Elroy, the youngest, had started clapping his hands, guffawing, and jumping up and down, which in that moment hadn't endeared him to McKenna, especially when the others had joined in.

McKenna was on leave from the credit union for the summer. She noticed Mayjean wouldn't fuss anymore when she went away. The older woman looked pale sometimes, but her reply was always the same: "I am well." Her weight was steadily dropping. Even this morning, she had to stitch her favorite skirt. McKenna couldn't understand it. Life was good for them, Mayjean seemed contented, yet something felt wrong, out of sorts somehow.

Summer also meant the busy tourist season had commenced in Belantine. Huge cruise ships filled with vacationers lined the dock in the city. Tour buses and operators would meander their way around the island, taking the tourists to historic sites and other natural attractions. Chantilly had little to offer the intrepid vacationer; the village was a stop for provisions and information to the next exciting discovery. Occasionally the odd tourists would spend some time in Chantilly, most likely as a guest, although there had been a few times when vacation was tied into a thesis or a field study.

Parrot Beach was a long curved strip of land hugging the shoreline. Tall palm trees shoot up to the sky, and wild shrubs guarded soft black sand, glittering like diamonds in the sunlight. Tucked away and secluded, the beach was mostly quiet except for the gay laughter of children frolicking in the surf. Grace came running.

"Come see, McKenna, I've found some eggs."

"Eggs!" McKenna exclaimed, laughing aloud in merriment.

They were trying to pull one over on her, she thought. The rough Atlantic sea, which for the past couple of hours had held so much appeal, suddenly lost its magic. The group converged on the area where Grace had seen her eggs.

A river tributary fed into the sea. It was on the bank of the river, in a small depression where the water had eroded lay a nest of eggs. On close inspection, McKenna realized they were turtle eggs. Some were still covered by sand, but others had been exposed. It was quite a find; everyone looked on in hushed awe and reverence. Some of the younger children held up one or two of the eggs, twisting them in the bright rays of the sun. The texture of the shell felt thin and papery; the eggs were round and hollow, lacking in density and firmness. They decided to leave their find exactly as they had found it. The little interlude had happened so innocuously that, for some time to come, they would reminiscence about this day.

While the others ate, McKenna went further along the beach. She had strolled for a little bit. Some bushes barred her from the view of the others. She looked up and he was there. A pair of kind brown eyes held her transfixed. Neither of them moved; they just stared, drinking each other in for long moments. McKenna had never reacted to any male in this fashion before; she was rooted where she stood. In the moment, she forgot her own name. A sensation akin to falling enveloped her; she wouldn't cower. McKenna pulled herself up straighter; a crooked grin appeared on the man's face. *So this is what instant attraction feels like*, thought McKenna. She felt fear, excitement, and exhilaration, so many emotions tumbling through her all at once. The blood was roaring through her veins, and her heart started up like a jackhammer, palpitating, like she had been running in a long-distance race.

How did this stranger get here? she wondered. This beach was off the beaten track. From his coloring, it was obvious that the man was from overseas. He was tall and good looking too. The wind ruffled his thick black hair. He was taller than McKenna was, a good two inches, she guessed. His facial features were remarkable, the bone structure prominent.

"Where did you come from, beautiful?"

So he was into flattery.

"How did you get here?" she asked him."

"Like you, I walked," he replied.

"Well, I know that," said an annoyed McKenna.

"I have vacationed on your island before. This is my third trip to Belantine."

"Are you staying around here somewhere?" A curious McKenna wanted to know.

Before he could answer, McKenna heard the others calling to her. She turned to go.

"Wait! What is your name?"

"You can find out if you care to," she said over her shoulder as she left him standing there in the clearing where she had met him.

The others didn't know McKenna had met someone. She was very quiet and deep in thought on the return trip home. These unusual occurrences were becoming more frequent she thought. She was naturally intrigued by the man, especially under the circumstances in which they had met. McKenna wanted to know more about him. In his presence, she had felt restless and edgy, like something had taken over her body. The encounter had left her moody. She disliked this out of sorts feeling. At suppertime, Mayjean noticed the young woman was unusually quiet and picked at her food. Normally McKenna liked Mayjean's callaloo, which consisted of meat, greens, and dumplings; but more than half of the bowl remained uneaten. After supper, the women retired early.

During the night, McKenna woke up screaming; the dream had been so vivid. She could actually smell and hear the roar of the ocean. Mayjean soothed her and gave her some more tea. After that, she slept peacefully throughout the rest of the night.

In the early morning, McKenna heard Mayjean feeding the handful of chickens scratching in the yard. As she stretched, a delicious feeling of euphoria stole over her. She jumped out of bed and burst into song. After breakfast, she decided to clean the house. It had been a while since they had done a thorough cleaning. McKenna dusted and swept, all the while singing. Mayjean took a good look at her daughter and knew instantly that it had happened. McKenna didn't know it yet, but her man had come, yes!

Sunlight streamed in through the open curtains, and a light breeze lifted their spirits. The women buffed and polished; curtains were taken down and washed. Every corner and crevice felt the fury of McKenna's dust brush. Mayjean did what she could to help. Their little house consisted of three bedrooms. The women occupied two, and the other room was used as a storage area. The kitchen was an additional structure that stood on its own outside. A modern lavatory had been added to the main house some years ago. Mayjean's children had all grown up in this house. The original structure hadn't changed much. The living area featured Mayjean's colorful crochet creations, which were displayed prominently on end tables and on various surfaces.

Each piece of furniture had its own history. The grandfather clock had been made by one of Mayjean's suitors. The glass cabinet housed a fine collection of dishes, cups, and glasses. It had been bought with money sent by one of Mayjean's sons. McKenna's piano took up one wall, two couches were set up in a semicircle, and the television set dominated another section of wall. The older woman had spent many hours here watching television. Her favorite shows included *The Young and the Restless*, and she would wait up until pastors John Hagee's and Benny Hill's telecasts came on at nine thirty and ten o'clock, respectively. But McKenna's energy was infectious today, thought Mayjean. By lunchtime, they had enough. As it was Mayjean's custom these last weeks, she went to sleep in the early afternoon.

At first, McKenna hung around the yard. There were some trees in the backyard. A little bench had been erected beneath one of the older trees. In its shade she sat reading *Annie John*. McKenna was making some progress, after having started some days ago. She could identify with Annie; her relationship with her own mother was strained. She decided to put the book down. A sudden craving for tamarind balls, her favorite treat, assailed her. She hoped that Elsie down at one of the village shops had some. She met her grandfather Anthony at Elsie's shop. He was hanging around with some of the other village men. Anthony had been making more of an effort lately to get to know McKenna. He had invited her to the family's home on more than a few occasions. Time had mellowed Hilda; she needed the aid of a walking stick to get around. So she was glad when she had visitors. Anthony was telling McKenna that he wanted her to meet someone. Apparently, a Canadian doctor was doing research in the area. He had approached the Serrants because of their standing in the community.

When they got to the house, McKenna was surprised to look into the same pair of brown eyes she had seen before. The stranger was speaking to Hilda, McKenna's great-grandmother.

"John, this is McKenna, my granddaughter." Anthony introduced them.

In the early evening, they all sat around a low table on the veranda, talking and enjoying Hilda's watery orange juice. John had been studying the effects of diseases on the human body since his early years in medical school. He was on the island to study the islanders. He had heard through Anthony about Mayjean and McKenna's work, and had wanted to meet them. When McKenna left for the evening, she had agreed that John could come over to visit Mayjean the next day.

When Mayjean heard about John's visit, she was exuberant with joy. She took special care with her appearance because she wanted to look her best. The cancer had spread; the last tests confirmed she didn't have much time left to live. Last night, in her pain and delirium, she had taken two pills instead of one; the pain was becoming unbearable. She would have to tell McKenna soon.

John was a very attractive and articulate young man; he kept Mayjean in stitches the whole time they talked. They discussed the uses of the different medicinal plants found on Balantine, and John took extensive notes.

Mayjean saw how John looked at McKenna, and was comforted. He was the one. She could let go now; her daughter would be okay with this man. The older woman could tell John was firm, but he would be gentle with McKenna. The young woman would be protected with him.

McKenna looked at Mayjean and noticed how awed her grandmother was by the man. For Christ's sake, he was a stranger; they knew nothing about him. He told them he was the youngest of three children. His siblings and parents still lived in Canada. The first time he had visited Belantine, he had fallen in love with the unspoiled natural beauty of the island. When this opportunity presented itself, he had jumped at it. He had rented a small vacation cottage in a neighboring village close to the shoreline. The private space afforded him some freedom from prying eyes. He was in the process of setting up his supplies. John needed an assistant; McKenna's knowledge of the native plants and people would be invaluable. John broached the subject before he left, and McKenna said she would think about it.

That evening, Mayjean told McKenna she was dying from cancer. The younger woman was broken hearted; great wrenching sobs wracked her slender frame as she cried out her betrayal and denial. McKenna could understand Mayjean's reasons for not telling her, but to know the older woman had been suffering all this time—unimaginable. McKenna lashed out in anger and pain, the tears streaming down her face.

"How could you hide this from me? I asked you many times. You said you were okay. If I had known, I could do more for you," said a weeping McKenna. "Mayjean, I can't lose you."

"I'm so sorry for your pain," said the teary-eyed older woman, plainly upset. "It's no use to complain. What's done is done!" Mayjean gently said as she wiped McKenna's cheek. "The Lord giveth and taketh away," said a resigned Mayjean. "Hush now, my chile. Let's rejoice with the little time we have left."

Mayjean had always put McKenna first. That was the abiding love she had for her daughter. Watching the older woman, McKenna knew she was staring death in the face. It was too much for her, and she started screaming, the sound like a wild animal caught in a snare. McKenna felt her hold on reality slipping away, everything she had known suddenly out of balance; her world had tilted with Mayjean's admission.

Mayjean's soft entreaties of "I'm sorry, so sorry" did nothing for the devastated young woman. McKenna fell to the floor, her legs refusing to support her any longer.

"What will I do without you?"

"You will go on, of course. You have someone who will help you. It will be okay, you will see," replied Mayjean.

McKenna kept whispering "you kept it from me. How could you?"

"I wanted to protect you, my daughter," replied Mayjean.

McKenna wished she hadn't. She was so cold, and her whole body was numb. Cancer was the enemy. Mayjean had always been able to beat any illness in the past. Her acceptance of this disease spoke volumes. She wouldn't beat this enemy, not this time.

The reality had set in that Mayjean was dying and she didn't have long to live. McKenna's world caved in on her. In one moment, all her happiness had vanished, leaving pain and destruction in its wake. She knew Mayjean had done all she could to heal herself; Dr. Russ had been a last resort. Mayjean's ability to cope with the pain was a direct result of knowing which herbs and wild compounds in nature to use. Her teas had helped to keep most of the pain at bay. The robust woman who was always happy and singing songs, especially when she worked, was gone. Almost overnight, a deflated gray copy had replaced the picture of health and vitality that had been her grandmother.

Mayjean resigned herself to her fate, and a composed peace settled on her countenance. Keeping the news had been a burden. The relaxed movement of her face and body told its own story; she had let it go. Watching the life ebbing from the older woman, McKenna knew she had given her all; Mayjean had always been a fighter. There was comfort and defeat in that knowledge, thought McKenna as she watched the other woman from the shadows.

Mayjean now lay comfortable in her big bed, waiting for the grim reaper to carry her home. Everyone in Chantilly took the news hard. Christina had to be consoled for days. The nonstop procession of visitors and well-wishers to the house was starting to get to McKenna. She asked Christina and Grace to relieve her so she could take a break from it all. She found herself in the city, in the humid heat of the afternoon. This was what she needed right now, some time to be alone with her thoughts. Her life was changing; soon Mayjean would be no more. She could stay on in Chantilly, or she could go meet Ruby in Canada. It had been difficult telling Ruby her mother was dying. Mayjean's children were making preparations to come home to say good-bye. The tears started flowing unchecked down McKenna's face. Life was so unfair. Mayjean didn't deserve what she had gotten.

McKenna found herself close to a little restaurant. She walked in to find John well ensconced with a woman. He was sitting across from a lush Belantine beauty; they were sharing identical glasses of a tropical fruit punch. The woman was hanging on to his every word. McKenna didn't need another dose of reality right now. She exited quickly hoping he hadn't seen her. She thought she had been successful until she heard him calling to her.

"How is Mayjean?" he asked her when he caught up to her.

"She's okay. I needed a break."

John had been to the house again, so he knew the circumstances surrounding Mayjean's health.

"Come join me for a drink," he suggested. "I am going over some details with Theresa here. She is a doctor at the hospital in the city. She is helping me with my research. McKenna was tired. She was about to get a drink anyway so she accepted.

A bubbly Theresa left them a short while later. McKenna felt John's stare clear down to her toes. His intelligent eyes missed nothing. He unnerved her as he sat calmly, surveying his surroundings. He didn't have to try to hard; there was an effortlessness about him. Though John was in his late twenties, he seemed so much more mature and self-possessed. McKenna was attracted to him, and he knew it. Men and women always knew these things. It was in the tilt of the mouth, the lifted chin; in the over bright eyes, and in the small, tight smiles; that would eventually progress into nervous grooming gestures.

The afternoon was turning out much nicer than she had anticipated. John was asking if she would be his assistant. She had thought about it, and she was definitely tempted. She was bored at the credit union, and with Mayjean's illness, this was a more flexible option. Mayjean was drugged up most days now. McKenna didn't have to work with John every day. The plants he wanted, she knew where to find them very easily.

Mayjean felt John was the one. Well, time would see about that. McKenna willed herself to relax and soak up the afternoon. Soon she would have to return to the ugly reality of death and dying.

Chapter 9

Mayjean had a passion for healing others. It was sad she couldn't heal the growth in her own body. McKenna made her comfortable as best as she could. Christina took turns with McKenna in taking care of her mother, which freed McKenna to work with John some days.

They were in the bush today. In the early morning hours, they had trekked into the forested interior to get a special fern. John wanted to study the fern's pain reduction capabilities. It had to be harvested when it was still cool in the bush. They had placed the uprooted plant in a plastic container and sat to eat a midmorning snack. Suddenly, a concerned look came over John's face.

"Don't move," he mouthed to McKenna. In slow motion, he picked up a stick lying on the ground; and in a quick upward motion, he had dislodged a midsize snake sitting on a branch close to McKenna.

"You know we don't have poisonous snakes here," said a slightly mocking McKenna.

"Next time I'll let the snake have you then," replied John.

They were very comfortable with each other. The excitement and sense of danger McKenna felt was still there though, just waiting under the surface. John was very calm and charming; it was in the little things he did. He cared about others; it was evident in the way he interacted with the people. The village children had taken an instant liking to him. Even the adults brought him presents of fruits and anything that they thought would be useful. He looked right at home in Belantine. Last night they had talked for hours, sitting on Mayjean's verandah, under a benevolent moon.

McKenna couldn't believe how much they had in common. He shared her passion for books and music; they had read some of the same books. Slowly but surely, she was falling for John. This expansive feeling had been described for eons by the great poets. Elizabeth Barrett Browning's decision to defy her father in order to experience this bliss resonated with McKenna. Love made fools and believers out of men. McKenna finally understood some of the mystery; this chemistry between male and female—it was electric.

Mayjean passed away peacefully in her sleep. Even though McKenna knew her death had been inevitable, she wasn't prepared. Mayjean had known though her time had come. After she had eaten her last supper, she had called her children and grandchildren together and urged them to do good always. McKenna was inconsolable; she cried on and off for three days. Her eyes were puffy and swollen. She couldn't bring herself to go see Mayjean in the morgue. The whole village was in mourning, May jean had touched many lives. Her legacy would live on in the love she had shared. She had brought hope to many, sometimes even when they had given up hoping themselves. She would be missed dearly. McKenna felt the lost most acutely.

On the day of the funeral, Mayjean's house was filled to bursting—if only the woman had received half of that outpouring of love when she lived. People always waited until death claimed life before they realized how much the deceased meant to them.

Mayjean had no idea that she was well loved. Village women came out to support the mourners. They set about making wreaths and garlands. The whole time, they sang songs of praise and worship to the great Creator, which lifted the spirits of all present. Mayjean's favorite song, *"Bridge over troubled water"* was sung in her honor. McKenna was overwhelmed by it all.

During the procession to the church, Mayjean's constant companion was supported on both sides by her grandfather Anthony Serrant and by Bepto. People Mayjean had known came from all over the island to pay their final respects. It was a beautiful service; not a dry eye could be found anywhere. Pastor Henry's eulogy captured the unique essence of Mayjean's existence. Throughout the reading, the broken sobs intensified, along with soft, whispered entreaties of the close friends and family. Christina suddenly wailed in distress and collapsed. Her husband, Mark, and some friends rushed her home, her belly still swollen with child.

Afterward the coffin was placed into the ground. In a daze, McKenna heard the pastor say "ashes to ashes." A slight drizzle had started, gently caressing the mourners. Some people said it was Mayjean's showers of blessing from heaven.

The mourners stood in a circle around Mayjean's final resting place. They sang a series of sad, mournful dirges, accompanied by the heaping shovels of dirt being thrown onto the casket. A feeling of peace and serenity enveloped the crowd; there was something special about Mayjean's funeral. McKenna was moved by the outpouring of love. It would be difficult living without her grandmother. The older woman had high expectations for her, and she had better live up to them. McKenna did not want to disappoint the woman who had given her so much. The salvation of the Samuel clan rested solely on her young shoulders.

Mayjean had left most of her possessions to McKenna, which wasn't surprising. The older woman had invested her money in a bank in the city, and Christina got a handsome payout. Mayjean's other children had their own means and did not feel slighted in the least. Out of all Mayjean's children, Ruby stayed for two more weeks after the funeral. She wanted to visit and get to know McKenna better. Ruby's daughters were very polite and enjoyed going on trips around the island with McKenna. It was good to have the extra company; soon she would be on her own.

Christina's had offered to come over sometimes, but she was in the final stages of her pregnancy and would deliver any day now. Besides, Christina had her hands full with her husband and children; she wouldn't be able to help anyone. McKenna would have to fend for herself. It wasn't the loneliness that scared her. It was the frailty of life, she always had Mayjean.

The woman had been bigger than life itself. The thought that Mayjean would be gone had never crossed her mind. McKenna would have to adjust to the new situation. Who would have thought that the other woman would have been taken from her so suddenly?

    Yesterday, she had ran inside the house calling out to Mayjean, only to be brought up short when the painful memories of loss had assailed her yet again.

Part II

Chapter 10

Life had settled down to a more predictable routine. McKenna began making plans to go visit Ruby in Canada. After Mayjean's passing, the villagers had been extremely kind and supportive. Beverly had ingratiated herself in McKenna's good graces again. The village men still had their eye on McKenna; some thought she would be easy picking now that Mayjean was no longer there to fend them off. John had released McKenna from his employ for some time now. He knew she needed time to grieve and heal. Most times, when he was in the village, he would watch her as she went about her business, but he kept his distance. He knew the pain of loss and suffering firsthand; he had come to the island in an attempt to escape his own pain. The island was very therapeutic; life was meant to be enjoyed here.

The weekend had come quickly, and John was taking a break from his work schedule. He had come into Chantilly on an errand, hoping that he could persuade McKenna to come back to work for him. An unspeakable joy filled him as he watched McKenna. She was like a rare and exotic flower. Everyone fell under her spell. She was unaware of the effect she had on others. From the bright-eyed looks bestowed on her by the other men, he knew he would soon have to make a move. Some of the men had given him some stares lately, but McKenna wasn't married. She was free to choose whom she wanted to be with. His work was coming along nicely. He was going into the city tomorrow to get additional data and to report his findings to Theresa, in the hospital. He thought he might ask McKenna to accompany him if she was up for it.

After chatting with the village men in Elsie's shop, John made his way to McKenna's home. Clive, a young man from the village, had beaten him to McKenna's door. Clive exuded an exuberant air of self-importance as he chatted up McKenna.

"Hey, John, come join us," McKenna invited. By the time a chair was pulled up for John, Clive had lost the charming but superficial smile that he had reserved for the other man. By his glowering and dour countenance, it was obvious that he was none too happy sharing McKenna's affections. Clive was a farmer in the village. He was looking for a woman to settle down with. McKenna figured in his plans, but he did not figure in hers. The three chatted over a variety of topics while McKenna poured grapefruit juice. It was evening before a reluctant Clive left McKenna and John alone. He knew instinctively that something else was going on that did not concern him.

McKenna looked up to see John smiling. Let them think she was some trophy; she had a mind of her own. She had no interest in being someone's plaything.

"So how are you coping?" John asked.

"Good and bad days. It's getting easier though. Everyone has been good to me," replied McKenna."

"That's good to hear. I didn't want to intrude, so I left you alone. Are you ready to come back to work?"

"I have been thinking of visiting my aunt in Canada," replied McKenna. We have talked about it for so long, I feel, under the circumstances, it's time I spread my wings. You know, leave Chantilly for a while."

"That's an awesome idea." John was impressed. McKenna was a nice surprise. She had a mind of her own; spunk was good in a woman. He would have to tread carefully here if he was to win her over.

In the village, there was anger building at John's presence in Chantilly. The grumblings focused on the attention that was paid to McKenna by the doctor. Clive had told the others about John's visit. McKenna was accosted and besieged daily about her personal affairs.

She was visiting at her old workplace when another man from the village accused her of preferring the white man to them. McKenna's blood boiled. First off all, it wasn't true; and even if it was, she was free to pick whom she chose. After Brian, she had promised herself that she would choose someone she was compatible with. If a relationship was to be truly successful, the goals and common interests of the parties should be of paramount importance, she surmised. She had watched Christina and Mayjean get hurt time and time again from making bad choices where men were concerned. She, McKenna, wasn't leaping blindly; she would take her time and make up her mind.

McKenna had applied for a visitor's visa to enter Canada. Her documents were sent to a neighboring island since Belantine did not process applications. When the postmistress called her name, McKenna had been overjoyed. With trembling fingers, she had opened the package then and there, and had squealed so loud. Everyone in the little post office had converged on her. By evening, the village was abuzz with the news. Christina was happy for McKenna. Lately, though, she would look at her daughter with a wistful smile. It wasn't that Christina was jealous; she just realized the chances she had let slip by. She had made many bad decisions and now regretted some of the things she had done.

The week before McKenna was to go meet Ruby, Christina gave birth to a bouncing baby boy she named Junior. McKenna was more than excited when she held the little squirming bundle in her lap. Mayjean would have been proud of the little tyke. Mark, Christina's husband, wore a proud grin; Junior was his firstborn son. Mark had helped to restore Christina's confidence in her self; she was a changed woman. It was as if love had freed her from the shackles of her past. As a couple, the two worked well together. McKenna was truly grateful for good men like Mark. His newfound family was his utmost priority.

McKenna had helped John sporadically while she got her affairs in order. The plan was to stay in Canada for six months before returning to Chantilly. Her happiness and excitement knew no containment; she was over the moon. This dream had been percolating for a long time now. John invited her to dinner at his home. After they had eaten, he said he had some news to share.

"Well, I decided to go back to Canada with you . . . for a little bit anyways. Who better to show you around my homeland than myself?"

McKenna was pleasantly surprised at the news.

"That's very sweet, but I will be at my aunt's house." She was unsure of how things would work out between them.

"Leave Ruby to me," replied John.

McKenna stuttered. But . . . I thought you have to work here on the island."

"Well, I have gotten quite a lot done. I am actually ahead of my schedule. All work and no play makes Jack a dull boy." As he said it, he tweaked her nose. "Besides I can continue my work in Canada, you know."

The rest of the week went by in a blur. On Friday morning, McKenna waited in the small airport with John and the rest of her family. The airport was just stirring to life. They would be boarding the first flight of the day. A set of plush sofas occupied the main area of the lobby. People were either sitting or milling around, saying good-byes and dropping off loved ones. On the far wall was a line of baggage handlers behind their counters and other airport personnel, checking and weighing in bags. The little airport was divided into sections: One of two snack bars was open for business further down. There was an area cordoned off behind a glass corridor. Beyond was immigration, and the lounge area for passengers boarding the plane. Christina and her family took up residence down the hallway. From their vantage point, they could see planes landing and taking off.

McKenna was impatient for the journey to start. Her stomach felt unsettled, as she hadn't eaten any breakfast. In her nervous state, she didn't think the food would stay in the confines of her stomach. John squeezed her hand reassuringly, sensing the nervous tension; he knew it was her first big trip. McKenna was glad he was journeying with her. She leaned into his solid strength, his bigger body absorbing her weight effortlessly.

The voice on the intercom barked out that it was time for boarding. McKenna said her good-byes to her family as she followed the procession inside the cordoned-off unit. Tears had begun streaming down Christina's cheek, and McKenna averted her head.

McKenna sat next to John; she had taken the window seat. Looking out from the window, the lush beauty of Belantine was seductive. Low-lying clouds shrouded the mountaintops, and greenery poked out from the dense vegetation. On the other side, the deep azure blue of the sea created a surreal atmosphere. McKenna felt a pang of homesickness. Mayjean's death was so vivid in her memory. Bereft and buffeted by her emotions, she was overwhelmed.

As her island receded under the plane, the tears came fast and silent. She didn't know she had been holding so much in. John gave her a wordless hug. In this moment, she felt so close to him. A sense of déjà vu enveloped her; this seemed so natural and so right, as if they had done this many times before.

They had one stopover to change planes and refuel. McKenna fell asleep during the rest of the flight. She awoke to John gently shaking her awake. They had arrived in Toronto.

The sheer size of the airport boggled her mind. Everything here was huge. McKenna felt out of her element. A ringing in her ears as they popped after the long flight unnerved her. She became aware of a loud buzz coming from all the chatter going on around her as people of every creed and color grabbed their bags and rushed to be first in line to clear immigration. In the early evening, the lights were many and blinding. McKenna felt lost in the throngs of people. Life in Balantine hadn't prepared her for this. For the umpteenth time, she was glad for John's company.

Ruby and her family, waiting in the reception area, welcomed her with hugs and kisses. John's brother had come to collect him. On the plane, John had told McKenna that he had his own home in the city. After everyone had been introduced, John said his good-byes and assured McKenna that he would be calling in a couple of days. Ruby lived on a quiet cul-de-sac, away from the heavy traffic of the city. Her home was a detached red-bricked structure framed by beautiful landscaping. In the darkness, the topiary shrubs looked like real animals and little people. Ruby had done well for herself; she had migrated when she had still been a young girl. She worked in the hospital and had worked herself up to a senior nursing position, which afforded her some perks. Her two daughters still lived at home. Ruby's husband was easygoing and laid back. He stayed in the background most of the time.

The house was quite comfortable, thought McKenna, compared to her humble abode back in Chantilly. The house was divided into two levels: the bedrooms were upstairs, and the living room and kitchen on the main floor. The kitchen was large and airy, and contained a seating area where the family took their meals. She was given her own room toward the back of the house. McKenna was tired and jet lagged. Ruby checked in on her before she fell asleep.

McKenna woke up panting; the dream had visited her yet again. In the dream, McKenna was being chased by someone on horseback. She herself was on a horse. They always rode close to the sea, kicking up the foamy water in their wake. The dream left her confused. She had never ridden a horse in her life. McKenna realized that she dreamed when she was experiencing stress. Ruby had planned to take her shopping and sightseeing downtown. The next day, a tired McKenna came down, ready for a new adventure.

Ruby took McKenna downtown, in the heart of the busy modern metropolis. They had taken the underground subway; Ruby disliked driving downtown in the traffic congestion. The car in which they sat was partly full. About five seats away, some teenagers occupied the other end. Considering the time of day, they should have been in school. Not fooling around, most likely playing hokey from school. Their voices were loud and obnoxious in the confined space, and their stance reeked of false bravado.

As the women surfaced from underground, the sunlight reflecting off the glass of the lavish buildings blinded McKenna briefly. Humanity was on the move, in the many vehicles that jammed the streets. The profusion of taxicabs, buses, and streetcars seemed nonstop. An impatient cabbie was annoyed they chose to cross the street; he had wanted to turn on the red light. The traffic and the din it caused bordered on confusion but it all flowed seamlessly. McKenna likened it to ordered chaos.

As they progressed along the downtown corridor, McKenna gazed into some of the most exclusive retail shops she had ever seen. The eclectic mix of art galleries, antiques stores, restaurants, and cafés beguiled and beckoned.

Ruby took McKenna into one of the quieter boutiques that lined the street. The proprietor greeted them affectionately. The sale prices were exorbitant. When McKenna hesitated, Ruby indulged her, so McKenna enjoyed herself immensely. She had longed for some pretty clothes, and she was finally getting them. Life was good. After they had visited a few more stores, they headed for lunch. It was a beautiful day, and the sky was completely void of clouds. McKenna caught glimpses of appreciative smiles from men as they passed her in the streets.

Such diverse cuisines existed in the city. McKenna didn't know which to try first. Sushi and pizza were at the top of her priority list to try. Her weight had never been an issue for her; she had been blessed with good genes. Like on Belantine, the city was a melting pot of the many cultures that called Toronto home. The exotic had become commonplace in the mosaic here.

For lunch, they ate in an authentic Italian restaurant. McKenna had never tasted finer pasta. The side dish was a mixture of vegetables, including roasted eggplant and endive drizzled with olive oil. The young waiter was very attentive and suggested they try some dessert. McKenna tasted pear sorbet for the first time. After lunch, McKenna jokingly said to Ruby, in the presence of the waiter, "I have eaten enough food for a week." She was that full.

Ruby's friends all wanted to meet McKenna. The phone rang off the hook for a good hour after they came home. A barbecue was decided on for the weekend. Later in the afternoon, John called for McKenna. They agreed to take in a movie in the evening.

"Is he your boyfriend?" Ruby asked McKenna. "No, not really. Well, to be honest . . . there is something, but we haven't explored it," replied McKenna.

"He seems to have his priorities straight," said Ruby. "In fact, I like him very much. You should grab him before someone else does!"

"I'm just taking it slowly. We'll see what develops." McKenna chucked her aunt playfully.

McKenna was awed by all she had seen so far. Everything in Toronto was on a bigger scale compared to Chantilly. Life was much more relaxed where she came from; it seemed that people in the city never slept. Upon hearing the constant beep of sirens, she had asked her cousins what was making the noises. McKenna was shocked to learn it was the emergency vehicles. The ambulances and the police cars went on all day long. Much to her delight, she had found out that she didn't have to boil water to take a hot bath. While McKenna was enjoying herself immensely, it was too soon to know if she was cut out for city life.

The movie theater was a housed in a huge shopping complex. People stood in long lines waiting to get tickets and snacks from the concession stands. John looked devastatingly handsome. In the cool of the evening, he had worn a black jacket and light tan pants. McKenna yearned to run her hand through his wavy black hair. His white shirt stood out in sharp contrast to the black of his ensemble. The looks were not only for McKenna; John caused a few rapid heartbeats himself. McKenna was attired in black jeans and a colored blouse, which accentuated her svelte physique. McKenna stumbled in the muted light of the theater. John steadied her. They took seats all the way in the back. He had suggested they watch Tyler Perry's film *Madea's Family Reunion*. The young couple laughed heartily along with the rest of the audience at Madea's crazy antics on screen. John would do anything for his McKenna. He knew the movie would make her happy. She had grown up with Mayjean, a woman of similar temperament to Madea.

John took McKenna to a little café after the movie. He marveled at his good fortune. He had fallen hard—hook, line, and sinker. McKenna was so different from the women he had known; there was a quite strength about her. Not a mean bone resided in her body. Her innocent, open countenance held no deceit. In this moment, she was unguarded, soaking up the new surroundings. John was not sure when he fell in love with her. Maybe it was the first he saw her on that beach. She had been a vision in her one-piece bathing suit, her thick hair curling around her beautiful features. He knew he could not live without her; she was a fragile rose in his parched desert. In the low lighting, McKenna looked entrancing, and John enjoyed the play of shadows in her eyes. McKenna had the most beautiful eyes he had ever seen. They were living liquid pools sucking him under.

He reached over and took her hand in his. Under her skin, her pulse beat in a staccato rhythm. She looked at him, fear of the unknown and uncertainty in her eyes. A dull flush had suffused John's skin; his breathing was a little bit on the choppy side.

"McKenna, there is no fear. It's just us sitting here," John whispered. The man and the woman looked directly at each other. McKenna knew in that moment, with all her senses fully engaged, that they would never be the same again. An irretrievable leap had been taken; they would be together. It was useless talking herself out of it. McKenna only had appetite for tea; she was on edge the whole time they sat there. In the background, a jukebox belted out some jazz numbers. Secluded in the corner, McKenna and John ignored the rest of the world. They had eyes only for each other. The moment was broken by the server. McKenna sipped her tea in hushed silence, refusing now to meet John's eyes. She needed time to process her thoughts. John took it all in stride; he was the more experienced one.

Chapter 11

Ruby's friends sat around on the patio. The grill had been fired up, and wisps of smoke wafted upward. The air was redolent with the sweet smell of roasting meat. Earlier in the day, McKenna had helped Ruby and the girls prepare the food for the evening festivities. Smells of Caribbean potato pudding, macaroni pie, salads, and rich pumpkin soup made mouths water. The delicious aroma wound its way outside and down the entire street. A gigantic potato salad, resplendent with colorful vegetables, sat in the middle of the round table. The other dishes were arranged around the centerpiece. Most of the guests were of Caribbean heritage. Ruby's daughters had invited some of their friends from work. The neighbors invited themselves over; everyone liked a party when the food was free.

McKenna hadn't done much partying before, but the mood was infectious, and she went along with it. Ruby's best friend, Grace, a rotund little lady with short red hair, called McKenna over.

"I knew your grandmother, chile. Sweet lady—I'm sorry to hear of her passing." She wanted to know if McKenna was enjoying Canada. They agreed that McKenna would visit with her before she went back to the Caribbean. Ruby proudly showed off her niece to everyone present. Some people had brought little gifts for McKenna. At one point in the evening, the crowd gathered in the center of Ruby's living room, the music was cranked up, and people got down to dancing. No one wanted the party to end; it was well past midnight before the first person said their good-byes.

After McKenna retired for the night, her thoughts turned to John. They talked every day now. She wanted to spend more time with him, but her sense of self-preservation would sometimes assert itself. She had prayed for someone like John, but the reality was always so different from the dream. To dream was to hope, but in the realization lay the seeds of despair.

She remembered a time when she was younger and had asked Mayjean for her dad. Mayjean had been evasive; she either didn't know or wanted to avoid the subject all together. McKenna had broached the topic a couple of more times and had gotten the same result. Tonight, after seeing Ruby's daughter, conversing privately with her dad, her hand tucked into his, McKenna had felt a pang for the dad she never knew. She had so many questions: Did he ever love her? Why had he abandoned her? Was he even alive? She yearned to know who he was. McKenna knew the answers rested with Christina. She had given her birth mother enough time. When she returned to the island, she would get the answers to her questions.

John wanted McKenna to meet his family. She had craved new experiences, but she was definitely out of her element here in Canada. Everything was happening so quickly. The nervous tension would not let her relax. McKenna generally enjoyed people, but being put under a microscope held little appeal. Exhausted, she tossed and turned before sleep finally claimed her.

McKenna awoke drenched in sweat, with tears running down her cheeks. The dream had come yet again; she no longer fought it. In her conscious state, she realized that the dream was a vision of something to come. Each time she dreamt, the images became clearer.

In the dream, McKenna could pick out clear landmarks. This time there was a huge wall of red rock far off in the distance. The horse she was astride was running hard; she couldn't seem to slow him down. It was by sheer force of will she hung on; the other horse was gaining on her. She could hear the heavy footfalls and almost feel the hot breath as the big beast exhaled. Calm descended on her suddenly because she had seen Mayjean in the dream. "You will be okay, my chile. All is well. Don't fear now. Remember, I'm always with you." McKenna now remembered the words that brought comfort and gave her strength.

The next evening, when John came to pick up McKenna, he downplayed her concerns. He was convinced his family would love her as much as he did. How could anyone not love her? She was charming, beautiful, and intelligent. McKenna had trepidations about the coming evening. She took her time with her hair and makeup. Ruby helped her pick one of the dresses they had bought. The dress was a deep loose fitting navy blue. It highlighted the brown luminescence of McKenna's skin. Her hair was like a living silk curtain, which glowed dark and rich from a vigorous brushing. McKenna willed the butterflies in her stomach to be quiet. She had never been around anyone like John before. When he saw McKenna, he whistled his praise.

"You look gorgeous. Don't worry about anything."

On their way to his parents' place, McKenna fired off a bunch of questions about his family. John was the baby. His older brother and sister had their own families. They had all gathered at their parents' home this evening.

McKenna watched as John drove. He held the wheel with a confidence born of long practice. He was in control of the car. A force of nature, he was comfortable in this environment as much as he was in Belantine. John would always define his world; his circumstances would never defeat him. He was a man of integrity. McKenna liked that very much.

They drove for about forty minutes before they arrived at a tree-lined street. It was an upscale neighborhood; every house had at least a two-car garage. All of the homes were well maintained and landscaped. The house they drove to had an old world charm. It was built in the Tudor style. The high arches and ornate pillars spoke of elegance.

A knocker above number fifty-four read "The Cohens." An excited John said, "We're here."

McKenna's stomach did a series of flips. John reassured her that she looked great. The door opened to a shorter version of John. John's dad was in his sixties, bald but still in good shape. He was dressed in jeans and a dress shirt. Senior Cohen looked welcoming enough. He gave John a hug and welcomed McKenna by shaking her hand. He murmured a quick "nice to meet you, McKenna" as he ushered them forward. Voices and the tinkling sound of cutlery floated out of an area that could only be the kitchen.

Some individuals sat around a table, eating. John brought McKenna forward and introduced her to his mother. Elizabeth Cohen had smiling blue eyes. The older woman was dressed in black slacks. She still had youthful features. She gave McKenna a hug as she welcomed her. A man McKenna assumed had to be John's older brother sat eating a steak. He refused to lift his head from the plate, his indifference cruel and calculating. Something inside McKenna recoiled. John put his hand around her. He introduced her to his sister, and the woman shook McKenna's hand in greeting. Another woman sat around the table. She was introduced as a distant relative of the family. Her distaste of McKenna was evidence by the cold haughty glare pasted on her face.

Chairs were pulled up for John and McKenna. The young woman wanted to turn tail and run, but she stood her ground. Her spine stood ramrod straight and rigid. She was a Samuel. She would not run from these people. They were hypocrites. Who were they to judge her? They didn't even know anything about her.

"So how did you meet John, McKenna?" asked Elizabeth Cohen.

McKenna got the impression that Elizabeth missed nothing. The woman knew all she needed to know and was just making small talk.

"We met on Balantine," replied McKenna.

"So what do you do?" the questioning continued. McKenna told them about her work at the credit union. They heard she was visiting her relatives in the wake of her grandmother's death. There was a small shift, a softening in their attitude toward her after that.

"McKenna's contribution to my work has been invaluable," interjected John. "Her knowledge of the medicinal plants on the island has been instrumental in the speedy progress of my research. In fact, today the board has broken new ground, using one of the compounds I found." John squeezed McKenna's fingers under the table.

Senior Cohen was proud of his son's achievements. He beamed at the youngest of his children. John had a good future, and he was going to do great things in disease research. His plans for his son didn't include this woman from the islands. He would humor their little fling for now, but he was certain nothing would come out of it. The Cohens' female relative was just waiting for her chance to upstage McKenna.

"John, where is Melody these days? Now that girl is going somewhere if you ask me." The woman let a sly smile escape her lips. A tense silence fell over the group. The woman's barb had been like acid, lethal with intent.

"She's around." John's voice was clipped and tight. He could have throttled the woman gladly. Who did she think she was, coming into his parents' home and putting doubts into McKenna's mind? His affair with Melody had been over months ago. Melody had dealt him a huge blow; her indiscretions had nearly destroyed him. John had found solace on Belantine, the island's natural simplicity and beauty had calmed his tumultuous emotions. After the woman imparted the information, she left hurriedly.

McKenna was introduced to the rest of the family. They seemed a tight-knit bunch. John's sister, her husband, and their two children were the most welcoming. It was obvious that John was closer to his sister than to his older brother. The younger generation readily accepted McKenna. She didn't relax her guard totally, but she felt more at ease in their company. John's dad told McKenna that they had a summer home on an island. They were in the process of making preparations to go there. Older Cohen was playing devil's advocate. He wanted to know more about this woman, who had captured his son's attention. The older man invited the young couple to come to the island, with himself and his wife.

Ruby was none too pleased when she heard that McKenna would be leaving. She understood these things though. It had to be done. It was always good principle to get to know the relatives of the person you were planning to settle down with. So she eventually gave the young woman her blessings.

"I will be back before you know it, Aunty Ruby. I still have a couple more months left of my vacation. We'll continue on when I get back." McKenna was convinced of this. John had filled her in on some of his past exploits. She had yet to ask him about Melody. There hadn't been a good time to do so. He had reminisced fondly about the childhood summers spent on the island. Prince Edward Island sounded intriguing. McKenna was definitely excited, and after all, she was an island girl herself.

Chapter 12

In the air, McKenna pulled out the guidebook she had bought, and read up on the island's history. Prince Edward Island lay off the eastern coast of Canada, nestled between the provinces of New Brunswick, Nova Scotia, and Newfoundland. The island was also known as the Birthplace of Confederation because the capital city, Charlottetown, was where the idea of Canada had been born. The bridge linking the mainland to the island was called Confederation Bridge, its curved structure, the longest crossing over ice-covered water in the world. A decade after its construction, the bridge endured as one of Canada's top engineering achievements of the twentieth century.

Prince Edward Island's first settlers were the Mi'kmaq Indians. They named the island Epekwitk, meaning, "resting on the waves." European explorer Jacques Cartier first discovered the island in the seventeenth century. Early European settlers to the island came mainly from Scotland, England, and Ireland. The Acadians, who also called the island home, had their roots in France. While the island was heavy into tourism, especially during the summer months, its mainstay was its agriculture, dairy, and fishing industries.

Standing in front of the Cohens' other home, McKenna was awed by the beauty of the surroundings. The house and the natural landscape blended beautifully together. White trimming complemented the various shades of gray of the waterfront abode. The home was slightly smaller than the one left behind in Toronto. It sat a little distance from the road, a centerpiece on lush green acreage. They had just passed a small beach within walking distance of the house, and McKenna couldn't wait to dig her toes in the sand. On the property sat several separate structures. One of these was a small stable and a corral. Instinctively, McKenna knew that part of her destiny would be fulfilled here. Fate had decreed that she should visit this place. One of the horses whinnied at that moment. The sound sent chills down McKenna's arms.

McKenna was introduced to the housekeeper, a friendly little lady who lived on the island. John was very fond of her; she had been in their employ for years now.

After a fresh change of clothing, McKenna wanted to explore. The older couple had retired for an afternoon nap. A walkout was located on the lower level of the house. Some white plastic chairs were stacked off to the side. A little path led down to some low-lying shrubs, and beyond was the beach. McKenna and John strolled in peaceful contentment. She hugged him back as he put his arm around her. McKenna felt cherished by John. She wished Mayjean was still around to see her happiness.

"So what are you thinking, quiet one?" asked John.

"Well, it's beautiful here. I'm just soaking it all in. From what I've seen of the island, so far it reminds me of Belantine," replied McKenna.

"I've decided to stay for a long month's vacation. I hope you'll stay with me," he said. "I want to show you Prince Edward Island. It's really beautiful here, and the people are very welcoming." John was smiling broadly.

"When I decided I wanted to travel, I never dreamed this would be possible, so thank you John," McKenna said sincerely.

John was a decent person. Even if the relationship went nowhere, she would always have fond memories of him. McKenna didn't see color where people were concerned. Color didn't defile anyone. She based her judgments on a person's character. John took his time courting her; he wasn't rushing her to do anything. Brian had rushed her because his only goal was to get into her pants. McKenna felt that if a man cared about a woman, he would respect her decisions. She was warming to the idea of settling down with John permanently.

Sitting on the beach in the fading sun, McKenna felt close to John.

"Tell me about Melody," she suggested.

John took a deep breath. She knew that he had been hurt by the woman.

"I met Melody in my last year of university. She was a beautiful and intelligent woman. We did everything together, especially as we worked in the same field. She is into disease research also. At one point, I thought we would get married. Our families pushed us along that route. We had worked together on a big project. Melody had always been ambitious and enterprising. In my wildest dreams, I never thought she would have done what she did. I never saw it coming! She wanted all the credit for herself. She had presented our findings solely as her own work. The director of our research department made her the head of a new division. When I found out what she had done, she had already started an affair with him. I was devastated. After the ensuing scandal blew over, I found refuge in my new work on Belantine."

McKenna listened, and empathy for John flooded her being. She had seen firsthand the devastation men and women wrought upon each other. Everyone deserved happiness. It wasn't necessary to live in pain and suffering. People were scared to be honest with each other so they hid behind props. The party doing the subterfuge always thought the other couldn't handle their truth. If men and women only understood they needed each other, there would be no need for pretense or deceit. Love should be about being open. Relationships needed profound honesty that would allow the true self to evolve. To love another involved a level of vulnerability and trust. The greatest pinnacle achieved by both sexes was in the shared energy of creating, the culmination that resulted in new birth and the blueprints for continuation, deposited into each replica of the human being. No one had to shortchange themselves for love. Love wasn't about self-sacrifice; the creator had already done that for us. McKenna was of the belief that we are all equal. We could always improve on our selves. But how could we change what the creator had said was already perfect?

"You made me trust again. I had given up on trusting women. McKenna, you are the light to my darkness. There is nothing with Melody. How could I after what she did. My aunt was just being mean and vindictive." John felt relieved after he told McKenna. It was good to open up to someone again. He knew instinctively McKenna would never hurt him. McKenna would never leave serious devastation in her wake; she had too much reverence for all living things.

They returned to the house and spent the evening in the company of the older Cohens. It was a pattern that would be repeated many times throughout the month.

Lynne and Gary, a couple on the island, grew organic produce for sale; and their operation also included a small chicken coop. John and McKenna stopped by to pick up fresh produce and eggs. The farm sat on four acres and was cultivated in a rotating pattern. Sections of unused soil sat bare and red in the late afternoon heat. Lynne was glad to talk to the young couple. Beads of sweat trekked down her deeply tanned skin. She had been burned a dark brown from hours spent in the sun. The woman's knowledge of the island history was vast. Her features lighted up as she reminisced about her years on Prince Edward Island. Afterward she invited them to a lobster supper down at her church on the weekend. The island was known for its seafood, and eating lobster dinners was more than tradition. It was woven into the tapestry of life.

McKenna wanted to see the horses. She had never told John about her dreams. Her urge was more than curiosity. She wanted the reality of the horses to affirm the dreams. Maybe if she saw the horses, she would understand—maybe even get a revelation. The stable held four horses. There was a black stallion, a beautiful white, and two deep brown mares. The animals stared with bright intelligent eyes at the intruders, their only movement, the swishing of their tails as they batted away irksome flies.

"Go ahead. You can touch them," John encouraged McKenna. He looked on in wonder at McKenna as she stroked a brown mare. She was naturally adept at soothing the animals. The horse was comfortable as she was, even nosing her hands and hair. "Would you like to ride her?" John asked.

"Well, I don't know. It's a daunting prospect," replied McKenna. "It's okay. I can teach you how. It's easy."

"We'll start tomorrow then."

John had ridden horses most of his life. He had learned how to ride from the tender age of ten. It was exhilarating to sit atop so much power. He had a feeling McKenna would grow to love the horses too. He pictured her, riding a top the brown mare the wind in her hair as she became one with the horse. John wanted his parents to like McKenna; she meant the world to him. He knew his parents were not sold on her yet. His father had excluded McKenna from their conversation this morning by reverting to their native language. He had been furious with the old man. They would have to talk soon. This was intolerable. McKenna and her family had openly welcomed him, and they had never hurt or embarrassed him.

The next day, John took the brown mare out of the stable and walked around the fenced corral with McKenna. He wanted her to familiarize herself with the horse's gait. For her first lesson, McKenna was decked out in John's sister flared but comfortable breeches. The pants had reinforced patches on the inside of the calves. A white long sleeved shirt was tucked in to the pants, and her hair was tied back in to a ponytail. On her feet was a pair of sneakers. It was the best she could do under the circumstances.

The little brown mare was a placid creature. John snuck her some sugar cubes, which she lapped up heartily. After they had walked for a while, McKenna bravely said she liked to get on. John hoisted her up on the horse's back. McKenna had difficulty relaxing. The adrenaline pumped through her; it was a heady feeling. Tension knotted her muscles as she tried to balance herself. They trotted around the fence a couple times before McKenna had enough. John promised to make McKenna a competent rider by the time she left the island.

McKenna loved life on the island; the people were the most welcoming. Life was more laid back here unlike the city of Toronto. The islanders were an industrious bunch; it seemed almost everyone had a backyard garden. When the couple visited friends of the Cohens, they would oftentimes leave with fresh produce. Agriculture was an important mainstay of the island's economy. The island's red soil was very fertile, and huge tracts of land were devoted to the growing of potatoes, grains, and oilseeds. The islands potatoes serviced many markets, international as well as domestic.

Fishing also contributed to the islander's way of life and generated huge revenues for the local economy. During the short summer months, when tourists flocked to the area, almost every establishment served some type of fish entrée. One of McKenna's favorites was the fresh clam chowder. Since she had come to the island, McKenna had eaten mussels and raw oysters for the first time. The fishing industry was rooted in the past, evidenced by most of the tiny villages that dotted the coastline. Most of the people lived off the land, which reminded McKenna of life back in Chantilly. She could easily see herself living here permanently.

McKenna basked in the glow of newfound love. She had been riding the brown mare consistently, and this morning, she was able to keep up with john as he trotted on the big white mare. She was amazed at how much easier riding had become. The little mare was like a special friend. McKenna noticed the animal seemed to look forward to their adventures together. She had started crooning soft songs in the animal's ear as she curried her down.

John was taking McKenna sailing today in a little inlet protected from most of the heavy wind. There was so much to see and do, and McKenna was absorbing it all. She had never been out on open water before. Unaccustomed to the rocking motion of the small boat, McKenna felt nauseous. The small boat bobbed in the strong ocean currents as the giant waves lifted and tossed it to and thro. Wisps of McKenna hair escaped the tight bun and tickled her face unmercifully. Wind sweeping through his hair, John was in his element. The deep blue water looked innocent as it eddied playfully around the sailboat. McKenna thought her swimming skills were no match for this current if they were to be upended. When they docked on dry land, the young woman couldn't have been more thankful.

In the afternoon, they ended up in the city of Charlottetown. It was McKenna's second trip since she had been on the island.

They visited downtown Charlottetown and Peake's Wharf, a busy, tourist-packed area along the waterfront. The couple joined others as they wove in and out of the many gift shops. The merchandise included island T-shirts, bright beach apparel, wood carvings, postcards, and historical artifacts, especially those from the native people. McKenna bought many souvenirs for her family and friends back in Chantilly and Toronto. Afterward, they joined the throngs sitting on the benches, eating Prince Edward Island's own Cows ice cream and enjoying the view of the ocean and a gentle sea breeze.

Elizabeth Cohen looked at the laughing couple coming up the drive in the early evening, and became troubled. As a mother, she wanted the best for her children always. John's happiness and well-being was important. Before he had left for the island, this last time he had seemed guarded and full of despair. She could see the changes in her son since he met the young woman. He was open, smiling, and carefree once again. She had automatically thought John would marry someone of their race. McKenna was a wonderful woman, full of humor, bright, and her beauty was rare indeed. She would never fit in with their circle though. Elizabeth wished John would come to his senses. Even this morning, her husband had been grumbling about the relationship. John seemed to trust the young woman implicitly. They were scheduled to have dinner at the West Point Lighthouse. Tonight, after dinner, she would have to sit down with her son.

West Point, constructed in 1875, was the island's tallest and most interesting of the square design lighthouses. In 1984 the house was refurbished and began a second career as a lighthouse museum, country inn, craft shop, and restaurant. Inside of the restaurant, a low hum greeted newly arriving guests. Attentive, knowledgeable, and efficient wait staff took orders almost effortlessly. The atmosphere was warm and inviting, almost like the gathering of a big family celebrating some momentous occasion. The restaurant on this evening was full to bursting, both inside and the outer patio seated patrons eagerly partaking of the good food.

While the modern restaurant offered a diverse menu, the Cohens and McKenna enjoyed a mouthwatering lobster dinner.

The Cohens were dressed to perfection. They were always gracious hosts, and their behavior these past weeks had been almost impeccable. Their smiles couldn't fool her though; she had been waiting for the shoe to drop for some time now. There was a certain forced cordiality. It was in the overbright smiles Elizabeth would paste on. Tonight John seemed in a reflective mood. Come to think of it, all day something had been bothering him.

McKenna had enjoyed these past weeks immensely, but she knew her time on the island was coming to and end. The time had flown by so quickly; she didn't want it to end. A rested and invigorated McKenna had not even dreamed once during the whole month. She would always treasure the memories of her time here. The islanders were a decent and industrious people. There was simplicity of joy here that wasn't immediately apparent in the city. Old mariners' folk songs and ballads that told of history and heritage were of immense pride to the people. McKenna had bought a couple of compact discs, and she planned on playing them to keep her memories of the island alive. Living off the land presented its own challenges, but the individuals she came across reveled in the toil. The benefits were more than monetary; existing in the people was strength of character that couldn't be quantified.

McKenna had retired earlier than usual; she came fully awake from her sleep. Thirst that was annoying and persistent assailed her suddenly. She threw on a pair of jeans and one of the big island T-shirts. Creeping silently down the stairs in the near dark, a sliver of light from the full moon shone down in the foyer, giving the furniture an ethereal incandescence. As she progressed into the living room, she could hear raised voices coming from the small tearoom off the living room area. It seemed the three Cohens were inside the small room, and they were arguing. McKenna froze in her tracks, her thirst now forgotten.

John's dad's voice rang out loud and clear.

"You're not marrying her—over my dead body!"

Elizabeth soft voice could be heard, entreating her husband.

"Bill! Don't be so harsh. He's your son."

"If he marries that woman, I will cut him out of my will." The older man went on further. "I will disown you, boy. You won't disobey me in this." The older man slammed an object down on the table in his anger.

The sudden noise caused McKenna to jump, the tears cascading down her face. She ran to the door.

"You see, there she is eavesdropping at the door. Bad manners, the lot of them, I tell you. I don't want them!" He smashed his fist into the table to emphasize his point.

"I wasn't eavesdropping. I came to get something to drink, and I was scared to move in case, oh, anyways, why bother." McKenna had wrenched open the door. She had to get out of there; she had never felt so humiliated in all her life.

McKenna was so agitated, her synapses were not firing on all cylinders, and in her emotional state, she jumped onto the brown mare and rode out onto the road. She heard John screaming. "McKenna, no, please don't!"

She was past caring, escape was more important than self-preservation. Scenting freedom, the horse galloped as fast as his legs would go. McKenna held on for dear life. Petrified and in near darkness, she started praying. The horse knew instinctively where they were headed; he didn't need the light of the moon. The wind whipped McKenna's hair around her face and into her eyes; the orbs felt on fire. Unable to use her hands to swipe at her hair, her movement was limited to staying atop the horse. She was fearful of moving her head too violently, and the errant hairs flew everywhere. So McKenna resigned herself to fate. Her hands were otherwise engaged, holding on to the reins as tightly as she could while the horse galloped in wild abandon.

The horse had suddenly crested a hill and started going down an embankment leading to the sea. Suddenly, it hit McKenna that she was living her dream. It was happening in real time. She could see and hear the roar of the ocean. As horse and rider came closer, the distinctive smell of the seashore comforted McKenna. In the distance, the brown red wall of cliffs beckoned. McKenna felt a sense of serene relaxation take over her whole being, and she stopped fighting the elements. She remembered

Mayjean in the dream, telling her to relax and let go, and that it would be all right. So McKenna did just that. It was in that moment that she heard the other horse pounding along behind her. She knew instinctively it was John coming to rescue her. McKenna's horse ran alongside the edge of the ocean, kicking up a spray of water all around them. The horse showed no sign of stopping or slowing down. A slick sheen of sweat and water made the reins slippery. McKenna could feel the hot breath of the big stallion as it thundered behind her. Suddenly the smaller horse veered sharply and started running along some low-lying bush above the waterline. McKenna knew she went flying; she was unaware of the moment when she landed. By this time, John had dismounted and came over to extricate her from the brush.

McKenna was covered in superficial cuts and bruises. John placed her on the wet sand and checked her over for broken bones, chiding her the whole time.

"McKenna, why did you do run off like that? I have never been so scared for anyone in my life. Please don't scare me like that ever again. I don't think my heart could survive a next time."

McKenna had gotten her wind back and exclaimed with righteous indignation.

"Your father is a vile man! I will not sleep in his house another night!"

"Hush, my little angel. Let's talk no more of this night," replied John. John stared at McKenna. He would give his life to protect this woman, and her value was far above rubies. He thought he had lost her when the horse had taken off. In the darkness of the night, it was good the horse knew the lay of the land. That alone had saved McKenna from breaking her pretty neck.

John thought it was sheer bliss to look on her countenance once more. He stared intently at his beloved and committed her features to memory; it was as if he was seeing her for the first time. The night was quiet; a serene tranquility permeated the atmosphere. The only sound was the two hearts beating in unison.

"McKenna, you are the flesh of my flesh." With those words, his head descended to hers. McKenna welcomed him. John kissed her with a passion lacking in finesse. It was the raw passion of undiluted adrenaline surging through his veins. He drank of her lips; the kiss was a reaffirmation of life. He tasted her for long moments. McKenna cried out her submission and her surrender as she kissed him back.

Chapter 13

Back in Toronto, McKenna enjoyed a few more days with Ruby and her family. John had invited the whole family to his home for dinner later this evening. Aunty Ruby wore a permanent grin these last days; she had spoken to John in McKenna's absence a couple times since they had been back from Prince Edward Island. It was as if Ruby was keeping a secret. McKenna was not worried. Everything would be revealed to her in due time.

The island girl tried soaking up as much as she could of Toronto before her return to Chantilly. McKenna had finally eaten Japanese sushi. The fish was prepared differently than what she was accustomed to back home on Belantine. In the islands, fish was always thoroughly cooked, but she could see herself getting used to the uncooked variety.

Yesterday Ruby and her girls had taken McKenna to the Toronto Islands. They had to ride a streetcar part of the way there. The distinct red and white vehicles ran on overhead electric wires and on tracks buried in the ground. A knowledgeable and patient driver explained to McKenna that the cars were an iconic urban mode of travel. Its charm was rooted in a bygone era but was still relevant in the modern city. The streetcar system had been relegated to the downtown core and surroundings in the aftermath of its heyday. McKenna had taken a quick picture with the smiling driver and had gotten some outside pictures too as the car moved off into the heavy traffic. She had enjoyed the ride immensely and couldn't wait to share with her friends and family all she had seen in Toronto.

McKenna had always been attracted to bodies of water. When she was younger, Mayjean had taken her to the beaches and rivers in and around Chantilly. The natural environment held healing properties that never failed to infuse her spirit with strength and support. There was a connectedness with everything in nature, if one cared to find it. Toronto was situated on the northwestern shores of Lake Ontario. Going to and from the islands required the use of one of three ferries. They had boarded on Queen Quay between York and Yonge streets. Sitting on the top deck, McKenna had watched the dock recede in increments; the built-up waterfront area in the foreground held her gaze. Faint strains of the Steel Pan music they had left behind could still be heard. The band catered to summer tourists and natives alike as people enjoyed the warm weather in the city. A slight sea breeze danced in the hair of all the passengers on board, and overhead, a flock of gulls cavorted, their outlines like shadows on the waters glassy surface.

Southward across the bay the islands, at one point were connected to the mainland by a sand bar, which disappeared during a heavy storm. During the 1800s, people settled on the island, and cottages were built to accommodate the summer crowds. Eventually, more permanent homes were built, and a community thrived there. The city, in its bid to create more open space for its burgeoning post-World War II population, had to reclaim the land. The islanders had put up a fierce fight, but by the 1970s, most of them had gone, allowing the land to be converted to public parkland. A small number of residents still lived year-round on Ward's and Algonquin Islands.

They had walked in the parks and on the beaches, whiling the time away. The birds, used to the stream of visitors, exhibited no shyness as they picked at numerous picnic lunches. In the afternoon, Center Island came alive with the sound of parents and children frolicking on the many rides. The Centerville Amusement Park was created with families in mind; over 600 hundred acres of parkland housed numerous attractions and food kiosks. Ruby and her daughters had seen it all before and laughed at McKenna's childish delight. McKenna was fascinated by the Gibraltar Point Lighthouse. Built in 1808, it was the oldest stone building in Toronto and the oldest surviving lighthouse on the Great Lakes. Decommissioned in 1958, the structure was steeped in suspicion and folklore.

McKenna enjoyed the time she had with Ruby and her family. She didn't know them well, and this opportunity allowed her into their world. She missed Christina and the others in Chantilly, but she had known them all of her life. It was comforting to know they would always be there. Mayjean's other children kept in touch, but they were always on the periphery of her life. The door was always open to them. McKenna knew infinite possibilities existed; positive thoughts made believers of men. At times, she missed Mayjean so much. She knew the older woman would be proud to see her coping and being strong. Her thoughts of the older woman would oftentimes result in tears running down her cheeks.

The family had retired late into the evening, and as a result, the entire house had slept in. McKenna was surprised to learn that Ruby's husband would be joining them for dinner. He had barely taken a break from his work down at the bank since she was here, and in his home, he was always very quiet. John had given directions to his home, and the dinner hour found them in the family's minivan as they drove there. John lived in a modern area on the fringes of the downtown. His home was part of a newer development. Tastefully painted in warm hues of sepia, cream-colored trim, and a deep red brick accent, it was a nice contrast to his parents stiff, opulent abode.

Inside, warm tones designed to soothe and appeal to the senses dominated. The carpeting and loose curtains invited touching. McKenna knew John would be nothing like his father. Bill Cohen was a cold, haughty, and domineering man. He ruled by controlling and exerting his dominance over everything and everyone in his sphere of influence. John didn't need to control anyone; his humble creative force drew people to him. People naturally trusted him. It was a two-way silent communication.

Looking at John across the dinner table, McKenna was very proud of John. He had taught her some valuable life lessons; he lived by an honest creed.

The scene of their last evening on Prince Edward Island played again in her mind. They had gone back to the house to drop off the horses and collect their belongings. A loudly weeping Elizabeth had greeted them in the living room; Bill was nowhere to be seen. She wasn't surprised to hear that John and McKenna would be leaving that night. After packing up their belongings, they were met by a swollen-faced Elizabeth in the foyer. She hugged McKenna.

"I'm so sorry, darling. Please keep John safe. I know you care for him."

To John, she had said, "Son your dad will relent. He will come around. Just be patient with him."

John had stood silent, never saying a word. His mother had hugged him tightly, unwilling to let go. Change had come, and Elizabeth was unable to do anything about it.

John had cooked a delicious dinner and everyone was replete. After dessert, they retired to the living area. Ruby and John winked at each other. McKenna sat in the corner of one of the two suede couches. A smiling John knelt before her.

"Will you do me the honor of becoming my wife?"

McKenna's mouth gaped open; she was stunned and speechless by the offering. She had thought about this, but never in all her wildest imaginings thought it would happen this soon. The others erupted into claps and shouts of happy laughter. After McKenna's brain had processed the information, she now realized why John and Ruby had been so chummy. He had asked the older woman. How charming and considerate he was.

McKenna was taking so long to answer that John had started to entertain doubts. He knew there would be no other for him; he couldn't envision life without McKenna. He was alive finally. Something had always been absent in his previous relationships. He now knew it was the connection between two people who loved each other. There was something special about this woman.

"Yes! Yes! Of course, I'll marry you," replied a nervous and giddy McKenna. John carried a little box. Inside, nestled on soft tissue, lay a beautiful diamond ring, perfection in the flawless cut. The ring was a token of commitment, a pledge of loyalty, a celebration of things to come. McKenna gazed in awe at the ring as her future husband slid it onto her suddenly shaking fingers. Looking into her eyes, John pledged his love. "I love you, McKenna Samuel."

Chapter 14

McKenna and John had arrived safely on Belantine shores two days ago. A teary and sad Ruby had been sorry to see McKenna go. The two women had bonded during their time together. Ruby had assured her niece that her door would always be open to her. McKenna had enjoyed the trip, but she was glad that she had Chantilly to come back to. There would be more travel in the future for her. This first taste had left her anxious for more. Christina and the rest of the family in Chantilly had met the couple at the airport. The family had congratulated John and McKenna on their engagement. Christina was so happy for McKenna her smile couldn't be any wider. John had kept his residence in the neighboring village and had proceeded there from the airport.

Jet lag could not dim McKenna spirits; she had stayed up late catching up with her family and friends. She had brought gifts for the children as well as the adults. The children danced around the room gleefully, showing off new clothes and toys. Christina's latest addition, baby Junior, had grown by leaps and bounds, his chubby baby face innocent of guile.

Beverly, Mckenna's old friend, had visited and was openly jealous of McKenna's ring. She told McKenna that her old flame Brian had gotten someone pregnant in the city and was planning to get married. McKenna flinched at the mention of the man's name.

After everyone had departed, McKenna contemplated her surroundings. The house felt empty without her grandmother's presence filling it up. Mayjean's death weighed heavily on her heart. Her grandmother would never get to hear about her adventures. She had shared everything with the older woman. Life wouldn't be the same, but she had John now to help her chase away the darkness. Sleep had eluded the young woman, but she knew she would dream this night. McKenna had accepted that the dreams were part of her; it was a gift, a natural ability, intricate in design and simply essential to her existence.

In a dream, Mayjean came again.

"McKenna, you have grown. So proud of you. I am always with you, have no fear. You have to give what you have to the world. Promise me. Many are waiting."

"Mayjean, what do I have to give?" replied McKenna.

"You will find it, chile! It's inside of you."

With those last words, the woman had gone. McKenna had called her back, but to no avail. If Mayjean said McKenna had something to share, then it must be true. A loud knocking twelve noon the next day awoke McKenna. John presented his love with some flowers he had picked himself. McKenna's wild exotic beauty humbled him every time he gazed upon her.

John reflected on his dad's ignorance. Didn't the man know this type of love was rare to find? He felt sorry for his mom, Elizabeth. No one deserved to live with a man like his dad. This love he had found was priceless, one of a kind. He would gladly live poor to call this woman his. Besides, he had his own money, the research work paid nicely, and he had just sold his house. John envisioned a future with McKenna as his wife. They would travel around the world helping others with health problems. John couldn't wait to have babies with McKenna; their daughter would be a vision of loveliness.

"Sleeping beauty, it's time to wake up," said a playful John.

"Well, thanks for the flowers, my prince charming," replied a still groggy McKenna.

Their love had been tested by upheavals that had solidified their bond. It was a love of born out of substance.

The couple spent the afternoon just simply talking and making plans for the future. They were both impatient to get married, but

McKenna had to resolve the issue of her father with Christina first. Some people in the village had taken the news of the impending marriage well while others still harbored resentment toward the couple. McKenna knew in time they would come around. She would always do well by her people. John would help them too. She had never met someone with a bigger heart.

In the evening, after John had left, Bepto, Mayjean's old friend came up to the house. They talked in length about McKenna's trip and had just started in on a late supper when a loud wailing rent the air. McKenna packed up the food for Bepto as they both followed others running to the village square.

A huge crowd had gathered around one of the village women. Huge fat tears were obeying the call of gravity as they descended downward. The woman plaited her hands together over and over as she tried to console herself. Her physical beauty was marred by pain and suffering, life's fatigue laying claim to her still youthful features. Her partner had used her regularly as a punching bag and tonight had to be hauled to the local jail. McKenna was incensed at the treatment of the woman. She knew there were many reasons why women stayed in abusive relationships. Her heart reached out in empathy. There was nothing she could do for the woman tonight as her family circled her where she sat in the square. As she turned to go, McKenna thought, *beauty without knowledge is a handicap,* and promised herself to talk with the woman later.

The next day, McKenna invited Christina over. Christina arrived with Junior in tow. The woman was besotted with the child, and he went everywhere with his mother. The women settled Junior with his toys on a play blanket and sat facing each other on Mayjean's old couch.

"Christina, I really need to talk to you about something." McKenna was very uncomfortable and shifted around in the seat. She needed to know. She couldn't move on with her life not knowing who had fathered her. "I wanted to ask you about my dad."

"McKenna! No! Not that!"

"I'm sorry, but don't you think I should know?" replied a tense and nervous McKenna.

Christina sat stiff and unmoving. She bent her head and took a deep breathe. McKenna had heard rumors about her mother's past. The two women were becoming closer, but they had never delved this deep before.

"I know you are uncomfortable, but please tell me. I need to know, Mom."

It was all the encouragement Christina needed, and the floodgates opened. Silent tears ran down Christina's cheeks. McKenna saw the effect the coming revelation was having on her mother, and she teared up too.

"In my youth, I was a rebellious teenager," said a distraught Christina. "When I turned seventeen, I spent a year in the city, partying and hanging around with the wrong crowd. Mayjean had kicked me out of the house because she was fed up."

McKenna listened in silence, never saying a word as her mother poured out her story.

"For money, I began working in people's homes, cleaning and cooking. One of the families I worked for was a young English couple." Christina took another deep breath. "Your father's name is Bryce Stevens. At that time, he was a professor at the local college, and his wife, Elaine, stayed home raising the kids. They were a nice family. I loved their two daughters dearly. One night, Bryce came into my room while I was asleep, and after that, I never said no. When I found out I was pregnant, I was thrown out of the house. I came home to Mayjean, and she took you as her own."

McKenna took her mother's hands in hers and said, "Thank you, Mom."

"So what happened to Bryce?" asked McKenna.

"Well, he and his wife eventually fell apart." Christiana replied. "His wife returned to England with the children, but your dad still lives in Belantine. Your sisters come back to visit every summer. I think the women and drink here has gotten to his head. My friends in the city update me occasionally," said a now-relieved Christina.

"Have you forgiven him for what he did to you, Mom?" asked McKenna

"I think talking to you has helped. I was afraid you would judge me harshly."

"I would like to meet him. Where does he live?" asked McKenna?

"He has his own place on the outskirts of the city, in a little junction. "My friend Paulette, can take you there," said Christina. Time and marriage to Mark had mellowed Christina. She understood McKenna's desire to find her dad. It was a basic right that shouldn't be denied anyone. Christina remembered the pain, angry tears, and bitterness that had been her lot when her own father had abandoned her. She would not stand in her daughter's way. If McKenna wanted a relationship with the man, then she would accept it.

The conversation then turned to McKenna's nuptials. The younger woman had decided that she would get married in Chantilly. At the news, Christina's joy knew no containment. In that moment, her thoughts turned to Mayjean. Her mother had done well by McKenna. She wished the older woman was still around. With each triumph, the Samuel women rewrote a little piece of their history. The new loving relationships of McKenna and Christina corrected the wrongs of the past and restored some missing family dignity. A smiling Christina left a little while later, wedding plans floating in her head. Mother and daughter had come to a new understanding of each other.

McKenna disliked putting off what had to be done. She had come into the city today. Now Paulette sat across from her as they rode to the junction in search of her father. A little path led from the main road down through some trees. Paulette was telling McKenna about the dogs on the property when a loud barking started up.

"Rufus, Squibs, down! Stop this racket now!" Someone was calling to the dogs.

As the women approached, a diminutive man was pulling on some ropes that held the dogs. It was the same man McKenna had seen in the city the previous year. The man went round the back of the building, pulling the dogs behind him as they jumped in wild circles looking for more action. The home in white and cream painted undertones was covered on both sides by more trees. Charming, not ostentatious, thought McKenna. A verandah stretched along the front wall of the house. The sole occupant, an intelligent but surly middle-aged man. McKenna could see some resemblance of herself in the man. Bryce coolly appraised his daughter.

"Hello. My name is McKenna. I'm your daughter" came out in a rush. McKenna was never more nervous as she stood beside Paulette. Bryce sat unmoving in his seat, McKenna moved closer to the verandah.

"Don't put your foot on my porch, you hear. I never sent to call you."

"Bryce that is cruel." The other man had come back around the other side of the house. "Chile, come with me."

McKenna was rooted in shock. Pain, searing and sharp, lanced through her heart. She had wanted to meet this vile person. His blood was actually flowing through her veins. While McKenna was led away down the path by the other man, Paulette laid into Bryce. Their fouled mouth exchange could be heard over the din of the dogs.

The little man led McKenna back to the road. "The man is bitter and unhappy. I'm sorry you went through that. He has changed a lot. In the early years, when I first met him, he was content, but then he never drank."

As they sat on a slab of concrete by the roadside, Paulette came up. She was incensed to the point of tears. "I can't believe the nerve of that man!" Paulette was beyond angry.

"Pretty eyes, so tall! McKenna, eh! You know you share a close resemblance to your first sister," the man said excitedly. "I'm Pierre," he said holding out his hand. "That day in the city, I thought you were Dinah. You're a bit darker, but the family resemblance is uncanny. Dinah is in England but she will be back soon. I heard she found a young man on the island. Don't worry with Bryce. He will come around." The man was convinced.

McKenna wasn't so sure, but she had already forgiven her dad. McKenna pitied him. To be so cold and unfeeling spoke volumes about his character. She smiled as her thoughts turned to her beloved John. She had found the love of a good man. McKenna didn't understand why people lived in the past. Bryce was stuck in his own prison, a jail he had made himself.

Instead of mourning for the past, it was time to move on to new knowledge, new triumphs, and new discoveries. The future always waited for the brave and not the faint of heart. The women parted ways with the man and went back into the city.

Chapter 15

The whole of Chantilly was abuzz with the news of McKenna's impending nuptials. McKenna and John's wedding would be a village affair. Even the men who had been annoyed by jealousy had come around, realizing that the couple was meant for each other. John and McKenna had helped many in the village. In the surrounding communities, respect for John had grown. He was no longer treated as an outsider but now was often regarded as family. The future beckoned brightly for the young couple.

McKenna wanted to have kids, but she knew her purpose was in helping others. She could be more than a mother. In serving others, she found a fullness that gladdened her heart. John accepted that about her. She didn't have to change her dreams or ambitions. McKenna could just be herself. There was freedom in that. Working together as a couple, they would create lasting beauty.

Mayjean's little house was full to bursting again. Ruby and the rest of the clan had come for the wedding. McKenna marveled at the power of a celebration. It had the power to draw people and make them happy. The wedding was to be held on the upcoming Saturday. Weddings on Belantine always took place on a Saturday afternoon. It was an island tradition. That's the way McKenna had always known it.

A huge tent had to be set up in the village park to accommodate the huge crowds. McKenna and Christina were working around the clock to get everything done properly. John's friends from Canada had flown in and were occupying some of the little guest houses in the environs. It was a pity that his parents would not be there. Bill, John's father, still hadn't come around but John was not waiting for him to. John's sister and her family would be the only ones present.

There was a contagious spirit of benevolence in the air in Chantilly. Great love had done that. Society could always set up rigid rules and barriers, but true freedom lay in the sacrificing of self to the work at hand. Every good thing can and does work.

McKenna was nervous the whole week leading up to the ceremony. Her life would be changed irrevocably, but she was ready for it. Mayjean had said this would happen, so she stopped questioning a long time ago.

The day of the ceremony donned bright and beautiful. All of nature was in harmony. The other guests had a huge breakfast, but the bride could not eat at all, her state nervous and excitable. The women from the village would be doing all of the cooking. No one could remember a wedding this size in the village before. They set about each task with a deep sense of community.

One of the women braided McKenna's hair in soft little ringlets; half of the plait was left to flow freely, the soft style framing an angelic face. McKenna's calm countenance belied the feelings of anxiety and trepidation. In innocence, she didn't know what to expect from the coming evening.

All too soon, the afternoon rolled around. McKenna was helped into the dress Ruby had brought. The dress was a white satin creation, cut in the long traditional style, and fitted McKenna to perfection. A long white transparent veil and a bouquet of fresh colorful wildflowers completed the ensemble. McKenna hadn't spent a lot of time with John the past week as they had prepared for this day. She couldn't wait to see him. She would declare her love for him proudly this afternoon. It was a love that had been birthed in the fires of experience. Their union had already undergone trials, but they would stand, for together they were a strong dynamic unit.

The church was already full when McKenna entered. The bridesmaids led the procession of bride and attendants down to the altar. John came halfway down the aisle to collect his bride. Not a sound stirred in the building. A sense of peace and an aura or reverence permeated the atmosphere. Mark, Christina's husband, stood for McKenna's dad as he gave away the young woman to John's keeping. John looked dashing in his black tuxedo. McKenna couldn't have been more proud of him in this moment. She could hardly believe this intelligent, caring man would be her husband.

As John looked at his bride coming down the aisle, her beauty radiant for all to see, thanksgiving entered his heart and escaped through his mouth. He was blessed to have this woman call him husband. He would do all he could to make her happy. He would pledge everything he was for her care and comfort. He was the luckiest of men. McKenna was a rare jewel indeed. He couldn't tear his eyes of her beautiful face.

The pastor's voice intruded. "Do you take this woman, McKenna Samuel, to be your wedded wife?"

John's "I do" resonated throughout the church. McKenna's own soon followed. Not a dry eye could be found anywhere. The pastor blessed the young couple as he united them as man and wife.

After the church ceremony, the procession wound its way to the park for the wedding festivities. All the vehicles honked their horns as they paraded through the village streets. It was as if the people were celebrating royalty. A raised platform had been set up under the tent, and it was there that the new couple made their first speeches and took their first dance together. Below in the crowd, the rest of the friends and family sat around their tables enjoying platters of food and desserts. Afterward numerous people delighted in toasting the bride and groom. Happiness rested on every face. Weddings had a magical quality to them.

The couple left while the party was still in full swing. McKenna and John would spend the night in a guesthouse. The owners had rented the little space to them exclusively until they went away on their honeymoon trip. John noticed McKenna's nervousness.

"McKenna, relax. It's just you and me now, come on."

McKenna tried to reassure him, but her smile was tight and strained.

"You look beautiful, Mrs. Cohen. I am so proud of you, my love." John brushed his hands down her cheeks in the light of the bedroom. After they came back from their honeymoon, they had decided to live in Mayjean's house. They would adjust to other expansions in the future.

"McKenna, no hiding here it's the two of us, we did this together." As John undressed his wife one button at a time, he revealed his heart, raw in his love, no pretense needed. John the man told McKenna the woman of his love for her. In poetry and in words, he talked about the sins of the past of a hypocritical society and his hope for change.

You healed my broken heart.
If ever my spirit would depart.
Be comforted in what we shared.
My strength found in the laying bare.
Of all I have, my soul.
McKenna, my love, I'll follow where you go.
No sun, no rain, no wind strong enough to lay blow.
Our love will endure the test of time.
My world everything I am, incomplete without your essence.
Your light chases away my darkness. This feeling, immense!
I love you!
Fragile beauty incomparable
Woman of my flesh, you're able
To give me sons and daughters
Life—giving source, found in the rivers of your living waters.
Feeds the empty and barren deserts of my parched existence.
Harsh limitations, restrictions and the wrongs of our society.
Love triumphs over propriety.
You have forgiven us.
But you haven't forgiven yourselves yet.

"McKenna, look at me. Let it go."
"John! No, I can't."

"Yes, you can, precious."

The buildup left her shaking. It burst upon her in a marvelous explosion of light, blinding. A scream so guttural rent the very foundations of her being. It was a cry of victory. The past was gone. McKenna's cry encapsulated Mayjean's and Christina's sufferings and the choice Brian had tried to take away from her. Her cry was the cry of a woman freed. It was the first tentative steps of building a bridge from the present to the future. It was the dawning of a new era.

The End